Jules Prudence Rivière

My Musical Life and Recollections

Jules Prudence Rivière

My Musical Life and Recollections

ISBN/EAN: 9783337084486

Printed in Europe, USA, Canada, Australia, Japan

Cover: Foto ©Raphael Reischuk / pixelio.de

More available books at **www.hansebooks.com**

MY MUSICAL LIFE

AND

RECOLLECTIONS

BY

JULES RIVIÈRE

LONDON

SAMPSON LOW, MARSTON & COMPANY

Limited

St. Dunstan's House

FETTER LANE, FLEET STREET, E.C.

1893

TO MY WIFE,

AMY FRANCES RIVIÈRE,

WHO HAS BEEN

MY FAITHFUL FRIEND AND COMPANION

FOR NEARLY

A QUARTER OF A CENTURY,

I DEDICATE THIS BOOK,

WITH

LOVING REGARD.

CONTENTS.

PART II.—ENGLAND.

CHAPTER I.

CHAPTER II.

CHAPTER III.

PART I.—FRANCE.

MY MUSICAL LIFE AND RECOLLECTIONS.

CHAPTER I.

My parentage—Village life—Paris—My first school—My first watch—Death of Louis XVIII.—Chorister boy—The seminary—The revolution of 1830—The pillory—A drama at the Hôtel St. Phare—The cholera of 1832—Leaving home—Engaged as cow-keeper—Returning home—First engagement in an orchestra—A singular trio.

THE invasion of France by the allied armies in 1814 left terrible memories among the population who were so unfortunate as to come within the sphere of the military movements. Nowhere did the curse of war fall with more severity than upon the little town of Nogent-sur-Seine.

The three emperors camped in the plain of Trainel, a few miles from Nogent, whilst Napoleon and the officers of his staff took possession of the Hôtel de Jerusalem, the largest and best in the town. It was here a detachment of Prussians, who had entered the town by the Faubourg de Troyes, sought to deliver a document to Napoleon, calling upon him to surrender, but the infuriated populace seized the three soldiers as they were crossing the courtyard of the hotel, and threw them into a deep well, where they were drowned. Not content with this, the mob outside attacked the Prussians, putting the squad to flight, several being severely wounded in the encounter. This hasty and unwise policy of the inhabitants brought, as it was bound to do, retaliation, and retaliation of a prompt and terrible kind, for the following morning the town of Nogent was surrounded by the allied armies, bombarded, and pillaged by the soldiers, Napoleon himself being compelled to retreat, leaving the Hôtel de Jerusalem in flames.

The Prussians thus being masters of the town, the hotel proprietor, M. Edmond Blacque, with his wife and two daughters, had to fly for safety to the woods, but they were speedily overtaken, and when identified as the owners of the Hôtel de Jerusalem, the family were badly treated by the soldiers who brought them back to Nogent, M. Blacque, together with two of his neighbours, being shot dead in the yard of the hotel, and their bodies thrown into the same well that had served as the burial-place of the messengers already alluded to. M. Edmond Blacque was my grandfather, and it was in the Hôtel de Jerusalem, every stone and corner of which I know, that my mother, Reine Blacque, like her mother before her, was born.

My earliest recollections, therefore, are connected with Nogent-sur-Seine, for, at the time of my birth, all these events were fresh in the memories of the families that had suffered from the devastations caused by the Prussians, who had pillaged, burnt, or otherwise destroyed all they could lay their hands on. My grandmother's description of the condition in which she found her home on their return to it, after the tragic death of her husband, and when the Prussians had left the town, was of a thrilling and blood-curdling nature. The left wing of the hotel had been completely destroyed by fire, and that part of the right wing that had escaped presented anything but an inviting aspect, for it had been converted into a hospital. When my poor widowed grandmother and her two daughters re-entered the demolished building, they found what remained of it uninhabitable for the time, owing to the dead bodies that were strewn about the place; and these corpses were, most of them, in an advanced stage of decomposition. Often have I shuddered at the recital, by my grandmother, of the measures she adopted for the removal of the dead. As the ordinary mode of interment would have taken time, she engaged a number of workmen in the town to tie the rotting corpses between two mattresses, and thus corded into bundles, they were carried, one after the other, by a couple of men, as far as the bridge, and dropped into the Seine. To clear the house of the dead was, as a matter of fact, to clear it of all the Prussians had left, for it was soon found that silver, china, and valuables of all kinds had been removed, the lovely Gobelins tapestries, with which the walls were hung, having likewise been torn down and carried away. A few articles of broken furniture had been left, but nothing remained worth removal. Still, my poor old grandmother felt unable to leave the home of her birth, and here it was that, at the ripe age of 99, she breathed her last. I can

recall, as if it were but yesterday, the ruins of the Hôtel
de Jerusalem, with its charred beams and burnt staircases,
all of which were left untouched for many years after the
tragic incidents I have endeavoured to outline. The well
is still in existence in which lie buried the three Prussians
and my grandfather, and his two equally harmless companions (for these victims of the Prussian vengeance were
perfectly innocent of the attack made on the soldiers by
the mob, and for which they were made to die) ; and when
during the spring, at holiday time, I find myself in the
Department of Aube, I make a sort of pilgrimage to
Nogent to look at this watery grave of my dead ancestor.

My father's family also suffered from the invading
Prussian army. In a less degree, it is true, and without
any member of it meeting so tragic a fate as that of my
grandfather Blacque, though it is a well-founded tradition
in the Rivière family that my grandfather, Henri Rivière,
who was a notary at Aix-en-Othe, died from shock to the
system, in 1814, after the burning of his house by the Cos-
sacks. Still, he died in his bed, and at his death his five
sons, of whom my father, Sulpice Prudence Rivière, was
the youngest but one, and an only daughter, divided his
fortune between them. With his share of the patrimony,
Louis, the eldest of my uncles, bought a large iron-foundry,
at Labatie, near Toulouse. His eldest son, Fereol Rivière,
after attaining celebrity as a barrister, became Conseiller à la
Cour de Cassation, in Paris, a position he still holds. Frédéric,
my second uncle, adopted his father's profession, estab-

lishing himself as notary at Palis, a village some four miles distant from Aix-en-Othe, where he married, and had two children, Auguste and Armande. The third, Antoine, set up a hosiery manufactory, in partnership with my father, at Aix-en-Othe, where they had hundreds of looms at work, and where, I may add, most of the inhabitants are, in some way or other, connected with the manufacture of hosiery; the adjacent town of Troyes being the great market-place for this commodity. Odo, the youngest son of the Rivière family, became a farmer at Chalon-sur-Saône, and the last born of all, Felicitée, married Firmin Fouet, who was also a hosiery manufacturer at Aix-en-Othe, where, for many years he held the position of mayor. When I have added that the two Blacque sisters, Héloise and Reine (my mother) married two of the Rivière brothers, Frédéric and Prudence (my father), I shall have said all that there is to relate of my immediate ancestors, who hailed from that small, but very pretty village, Aix-en-Othe, which at the time I am writing of contained but 1200 inhabitants, though it counts more than double that number now. Aix-en-Othe, which is situated in the centre of the Champagne district, is picturesquely situated in the middle of the immense forest of Othe, and commands an extensive view of the surrounding country. Here I was born, on November 6th, 1819, at the top of the high street, and quite near the Church of St. Avit, and here the first three years of my life were spent. My mother, however, whose girlhood had been passed in more bustling surroundings, soon

grew tired of the comparatively primitive life of my father's
village, and at her instigation his share in the hosiery
business was taken over by my uncle Antoine, and the three
of us (for I was an only child), removed to Paris, where
my father accepted an excellent position as inspector on
the river Seine of the charcoal coming to Paris from
different parts of the country. All that, at seventy odd
years of age, I can remember of this period of my infancy,
was my left hand being crushed in a door, the mark of which
remains to this day, and the still sadder event of the death
of a little fair-haired baby girl, who was called my " petite
blonde," and with whom, as we were near neighbours, I
used to play. I was said to be inconsolable at this event.

It was in 1822 that we took up our abode in Paris,
my father being out all day in his business as inspector, whilst my mother, a most thrifty woman, and
always bent on saving for a rainy day, divided her time
between housekeeping and my education. The rainy
day came, as she said, too soon, for my father, owing
to his exposure to cold on the river, was attacked with
rheumatism in an acute form, and compelled in consequence to relinquish his appointment. It became a
question of finding a more congenial occupation for my
father, a matter that was speedily settled between him and
his brothers Antoine and Frédéric, my father conceiving the
scheme of a partnership in charcoal manufacture. The plan
adopted was that Antoine, who lived in the very middle of
the forest of Othe, should buy the wood, have it cut and

prepared for charcoal, and despatch it by canals to Frédéric at Sens, where it should be converted into charcoal, and forwarded by river to my father in Paris for sale at the various markets. The plan seemed feasible, and, at the outset, matters worked well enough, my father, who rented a large shed at the Marché des Recollets, on the Canal St. Martin, disposing of the charcoal as fast as it reached him. The success of the partnership unfortunately was but of short duration, for during the terrible winter of 1827, when the Seine was frozen for nearly a month, three boats belonging to the Rivière Brothers were amongst the many that, despite precautions, were completely wrecked when the breaking up of the ice occurred. Insurance, which is still but little practised in France, was then comparatively unknown, and the loss sustained by my father and his brothers was so heavy as to completely discourage them from continuing this charcoal partnership. So Antoine returned to his hosiery manufactory, and Frédéric resumed his former occupation; but my father, who had nothing to fall back upon, was glad to accept the offer of his eldest brother Louis to be manager of his iron-foundry near Toulouse. When he set out on this new appointment he left my mother and myself for a time in Paris, an arrangement that met with no opposition from my mother, as this particular brother-in-law had never been much of a favourite with her, and she was glad, therefore, to avoid coming in contact with him.

And so, when my father was settled in Toulouse, my

education seriously began by my being sent to school, concurrently with which event occurred my first public explosion of temper. This consisted in my point-blank refusal to kneel down and pray with the others. I had even the temerity, although I had not been in the schoolroom ten minutes, to argue the point with the master, by telling him I had said my prayers at home, and that till I went to bed at night I would say no more. Nor did the master's gentle persuasion avail anything. I was sent home again to my mother, who gave me the chastisement I had assuredly earned. There was no repetition, I need hardly say, of this foolish insubordination on my part, nor was any further notice taken of the matter when I presented myself in class the following morning. My mother, too, strict disciplinarian though she was, so completely overlooked the offence as to give me my first watch a few days after when, on St. Nicolas day, which is called the children's fête-day, I was taken with the other boys of the school to the Jardin Zoologique. This watch, however, was in my possession but a few hours, for on reaching home in the evening I discovered I had lost it. How, of course, I could not say.

It was whilst we were living on the Quai d'Anjou in the Ile of St. Louis, and prior to the incidents just recorded, that Louis XVIII. died. Child as I was at the time, I can recall being taken by my mother to the house of some friends on the Boulevard Montmartre to witness the funeral procession, which was one of the most

imposing spectacles France has ever seen. I need do no
more than briefly refer to this magnificent pageant, for it is,
of course, a matter of history that all the regiments
garrisoned in Paris—infantry, cavalry, and artillery—took
part in it; the hearse being preceded by the celebrated
Cent Suisses, and all the clergy of Paris, all the monks,
Capucines, and Sisters of Charity following with wax
lights in their hands. A dazzling and bewildering scene to
my young eyes was this last Royal funeral. Paris has seen
many imposing exhibitions of various kinds since the death
of Louis XVIII., but as the succeeding monarchs, Charles
X., Louis Philippe and Napoleon III. all died in exile, the
funeral of Louis XVIII. was, as I have said, the last of
its kind.

The next incident that I can vividly recall is one that
concerns me more personally. It was my admission, in 1827,
to the choir of the Church of St. Louis-en-l'Ile. This was
effected at the instance of M. de la Malmaison, the vener-
able curé of the parish, with whom my mother, who was a
particularly pious woman, was on very friendly terms. It was
whilst acting as chorister boy that I obtained my first notions
in music, and excellent practice this singing in the Church
services proved. I soon attained a degree of proficiency
that induced the choir-master to put me in the centre of the
boys as their leader, and I was not infrequently sent up to
the organ to sing solos. Here I remained for some time,
my mother, meanwhile, providing me with music-masters,
from one of whom, M. Courtois, I had lessons on the

violin, and it was at this early period of my life, when I was little more than eight years old, that the short-sightedness from which I have suffered to this day made itself felt. I was found to be constantly dropping the instrument to look closely at the notes, and so spectacles had to be provided for me. I next learnt the guitar from a German lady, Fräulein Hirten, though nobody quite knew why my mother selected this instrument. After the guitar I was taught the piano, and as, living on the floor above us, there was the organist of our church, a M. Desquimare, with whom we were on very neighbourly terms, I had every opportunity of making progress in my musical studies. My advancement proceeding, I was selected, in the absence through indisposition of M. Desquimare, to conduct the Sunday services, and so what with school, music lessons, and choir practices, my time was fully occupied. Having, however, neither brothers nor sisters, my boyhood knew little of nursery life, and I was able, therefore, to devote closer attention to my studies. Still, despite my perseverance, I was not successful in a competition I entered for a vacant post in the choir of Nôtre Dame. I was deemed to be the best reader of music among the candidates, but my voice was not of the requisite standard.

A little later than this, when I was about eleven years of age, I was sent to the seminary of St. Nicolas-du-Chardonet to study for the priesthood, it being my mother's pet ambition that her only son should enter the Church. She had dreams of seeing me become a curate in a village

—dreams, I need not say, that have never been at all near realization. However, the early religious training I had had at home was supplemented at the seminary by that of the kind old Abbé Mauleon, who confessed me, and who must, I think, have grown weary of the weekly recital of my failings, which, I well remember, were greediness, laziness, bad temper, and disobedience. I presume the old abbé argued that the fact of a boy owning to so much was sufficient proof that he was not quite incorrigible, for certain it is, he never hesitated long about giving me absolution. The Church, however, was evidently not my bent, and, if I had any at so early an age, it was for music, which, even at St. Nicolas-du-Chardonet, I was able to keep up, permission being granted by the Superior of the Seminary, l'Abbé Colonna, a relative of the Napoleon family, for me to remain in my room, during what was called recreation time, to practise the violin. I have retained a pleasant recollection alike of the professors and of the institution, in which I remained for four years, though 'I thought in those days, and I should probably think more strongly still on the point now if I were asked for an opinion, that an excess of time was devoted to prayers. It was during the early part of my stay at the seminary that the Revolution of July, 1830, broke out, and Charles X. was dethroned to make way for Louis Philippe, who was styled Roi des Français. The three days' Revolution of the 28th, 29th, and 30th July is as vivid in my memory as if it had only occurred last week. Being near the Place de

Grève and the Hôtel de Ville, we could hear distinctly the struggle between the Royal army and the insurgents. On the first day, when the Hôtel de Ville was taken by storm and pillaged, severe fighting was carried on in all the streets of Paris, owing to the erection of barricades at the street corners, which prevented the free passage of the soldiers. The cannonading that ensued from this created a din not easily forgotten by those who heard it. The victorious insurgents devoted their second day, I remember, to desecrating the churches, beginning with the Archbishop's Palace, which was completely wrecked by the mob, all the vestments, candelabras, and other valuable ornaments of the adjoining church of Nôtre Dame being thrown into the Seine in front of the Palace. And after the destruction of the valuable books composing the Archbishop's library, the Palace was burnt down, a sight I well recollect, being taken out by my mother to see it, for it was her idea that a boy should see all that was going on. The wisdom of her course, however, on this occasion was doubtful, as the following incidents will show. Broken-hearted after the scenes we had thus witnessed, from, I need hardly say, a safe distance, as we turned to go home we met a tall, wild-looking fellow, wearing an archbishop's tiara on his head, and clothed, altogether, in priestly garments. The ruffian, who was drunk, had a sword in his right hand that he brandished about in front of my mother, shouting the while, " Vive la liberté ! " to which she, poor woman, replied, by bowing meekly and repeating the words "Vive la liberté!" Her presence of mind, no doubt, served us in good stead, for we should probably have fared badly had my mother ventured to retort with "Vive le Roi!" Among the sights we saw on this same day was the destruction of the iron cross on the church of St. Gervais. This was pulled down by means of a long rope, the cross falling with a fearful crash into the street. The church of St. Louis-en-l'Ile we saw similarly treated, but this cost the life of one of the ringleaders. The man had climbed to the tower for the purpose of adjusting the rope, when he missed his footing, and fell a shapeless mass on the stones beneath. Nor did my seminary escape. The insurgents took up their abode in the building, and the pupils had to escape as best they could over a wall and go by a back street (Rue de Pontoise) to their homes. The large rooms, we learned afterwards, had been turned into a hospital for the wounded, and it was not until peace was restored that we could resume our studies.

Another terrible recollection I have of the same period is of the pillory. This I was taken to see just before it was abolished, not, as it might seem, because my mother delighted in morbid spectacles, but because of the persistent idea she had, and to which I have already alluded, as to a boy's education being comprehensive. The degrading spectacle was carried out, as many of my readers may be aware, in front of the Palace of Justice, near Nôtre Dame, a large wooden platform, several feet high, being erected in the centre of the square every Sunday following the Assize Sessions.   On this platform were fixed the poles, having stout planks like signboards on the top, containing holes for the neck and wrists, the poles corresponding in number with the list of prisoners condemned to the punishment.   At mid-day, a procession of criminals was formed at the prison of the concièrgerie, and they were marched in solemn file to the square, where, one after the other, they mounted the platform to be fixed, as in a vice, to a pole.   In aggravation of the punishment particulars were written over the heads of the offenders, setting forth their name, age, profession, and nature of the crime to be punished.   For two long hours were these wretched creatures exposed to the ribald sarcasm of a gaping crowd, which often enough pelted them with rotten eggs and other abominations.   I have good reason to remember the pillory, for it so happened that when my mother took me it was the last occasion on which women were thus punished; and what has engraven the circum-stance still more forcibly in my mind is, that in the two women we recognized a Madame Maurin and her daughter, who had belonged to quite a respectable middle-class family originally living at Nogent-sur-Seine.   Madame Maurin, who was the daughter of the postmaster of Nogent, was known by sight to everyone in the town, and when her husband, who also held an official position in Nogent, died, the young widow, with her only child, a girl, named An-gelique, came to Paris, where she bought the lease of the Hôtel St. Phare, situated at the corner of the Boulevard and the Faubourg Montmartre, now occupied by the Brébant Restaurant. The crime for which these misguided women were condemned to ten years' penal servitude, in addition to the pillory, was the more discreditable because they were not driven by poverty to rob. This, however, is a needless train of reasoning for me to take up, for physiologists would at once point out that our prisons contain but a small percentage of people compelled by necessity to break the laws of their country, by far the larger proportion being impelled to sin by instinct.

As a matter of fact, Madame Maurin and her daughter were doing a flourishing business at their hotel, when they conceived and carried out the plot of robbing Señor Ragolo, a rich Spaniard, who was one of the frequenters of the establishment, and who was known always to have large sums of money about him. By administering a narcotic to him one night at dinner, the mother contrived, when he was in a state of coma, to take his keys from his pocket, and going to his rooms, which she ransacked, she took possession of all the valuables contained in them. On discovering the robbery the next morning, Señor Ragolo communicated with the police. Suspicion, however, did not at first fall upon anybody in the building, and least of all upon Madame Maurin, until a thorough search being made, the stolen notes and jewels were found in the cellars, and the crime was traced beyond all doubt to the two women. It was a shock that I shall never forget, to see amongst the wretched convicts chained to their respective

C

poles these two women, whose features were so familiar to me as to make me for the moment think that they were personal friends who were being thus tortured. The mother, still a good-looking woman, was loudly execrated by the excited mob, less, probably, on account of her crime than for having brought her young daughter to such a position, for the beautiful Angelique—the beauty of this girl of eighteen was really remarkable — was the object of much sympathy, all of which clearly shows that even gaping idlers are swayed by sentiment. It is true she looked the picture of misery with the wind blowing her long flowing hair across her face and over her shoulders, and it was with a heavy heart we turned from the Palace of Justice to go home. My poor mother, who, owing to their having been neighbours, was quite unable to look upon Madame Maurin and her daughter as ordinary criminals, used to inquire about them when they were in prison. The mother died before her term had expired, and the disgraced Angelique, when the time came for her release, exchanged the walls of the prison for those of a convent.

Parisians had barely had time to recover from the revolutionary troubles already referred to when the cholera of 1832 broke out, striking down its thousands daily. And sickening sights, indeed, this scourge entailed. Paris has been so much improved during the past forty years, that my readers would never, if I devoted pages to describing some of the streets, credit the account I should have to give of them. I will, therefore, pass over the cholera outbreak by simply stating that, in the Rue de la Mortellerie, one of the dirtiest in the city, I more than once saw a long procession of vans containing the dead bodies of the people who had died in the night, the plan adopted being to throw the corpses out of the windows into the vans below. The undertakers sometimes missed their aim, and the bodies fell upon the pavement. It was a sickening sight indeed!

Children have a habit of denying that their school days are their happiest, and from their point of view they are probably right. But, looking back upon the terrible events that occurred during my early youth, I am bound to say that I was happier at the seminary than when I was sight-seeing with my mother. One boy's school life is so much like another's, that there is little worth relating of the time I passed at the Seminary of St. Nicolas-du-Chardonet, and, but for the heavy punishment inflicted on me by my mother for what was, after all, only a boyish freak, I should not think it necessary to relate an offence I committed that resulted in my leaving the seminary. My mother, after the habit of some mothers, had a fancy for having my clothes " made for growing," as she used to say, though, as a matter of fact, they were always worn out before I had grown to them. I was compelled, also, to wear quite flat-heeled shoes, and these I disliked because they looked like slippers, whereas the other boys, most of whom belonged to rich, and some to aristocratic families, were, generally, better dressed and wore smart high-heeled boots. The demon of envy I suppose entered my young soul one Thursday when I was to have a holiday (we were allowed to spend alternate Thursdays with our parents), and I resolved to go into the room where all the boys' boots were kept and borrow a pair for the day, which I did. That one wrong deed leads to another was true enough in my case, for, naturally, with another boy's boots on my feet, I was afraid to present myself at home. After playing truant all day I was caught in the evening in the act of replacing the borrowed boots, and this being reported to my mother, who at once said I had not been home, I was politely requested to leave the establishment. This severe measure was adopted by the schoolmaster, no doubt, with a view to setting an example to the other boys, but I must confess I was totally unprepared for the course adopted by my mother, in punishment of what she must certainly have considered a heinous offence. The next morning she took me out for a walk beyond the gates of Paris, and when we were on the high road towards Charenton, she stopped suddenly short, and handing me a basket with a few articles of clothing and provisions, and some money as well, she said, "Jules, you are a very bad boy, and so we must part. Follow the road before you. Go, my lad, and may God bless you!"

My mother then turned back, and as soon as I had recovered from my surprise I walked on, without, I am now ashamed to own, once looking round after her. She had shown severity, perhaps, but my own conduct denoted not a little callousness. I walked on for some distance till, in fact, I began to feel tired, and then my pent-up feelings found relief in a good cry, and I sat under a tree by the road-side (it was a glorious spring morning) and began to consider my position. It was, altogether, an eventful day for me, for, during a terrible storm that occurred soon after I had devoured the eatables contained in the basket, I should have been almost washed away, but for the shelter offered me by some men who were driving a van along the road, and who stopped by the wayside to take shelter under their van, such was the violence of the storm. By nightfall, when I had walked about fifteen miles, I found myself in the town of Brie Comte-Robert, noted for its cheese, and here it was I put up for the night at an inn frequented by rather rough-looking peasants, who did not attempt to disguise the amusement my long black school coat caused them. Their manner, however, was kind, so kind, in fact, that I was very soon encouraged to tell them my story, as well as my determination to seek employment of some sort. "You will never get anything to do, my boy, with that long black coat on your back," said one of the party, and, in a very few minutes, I was induced to let him cut it a good bit shorter, and then, after a hearty supper, I was glad to seek rest in the scantily furnished room allotted to me by the good-hearted landlady of the place. Good-hearted, indeed, she must have been, for how else was the generosity to be explained which induced her, not only to forego making any charge for the accommodation I had had, but to insist upon my accepting a small sum of money, as well as a fresh stock of provisions for my basket. It was, therefore, with a comparatively light heart I set out in search of a situation, but as the inquiries I made in the centre of the town of Brie resulted in nothing, it occurred to me to apply at the barracks to see if the Gendarmes could give me a hint of any kind. Here, again, I had the same advice as that given by the friendly landlady, who had tried to persuade me to go back to my mother. All to no purpose, however, and I was about once more to proceed on my journey, when the sergeant, calling me back, told me if I was not too proud to accept a cow-boy's place he knew where such a boy was wanted. This, I need hardly say, did not sound like the realization of my dreams, but not being in a position to be proud there was little choice left to me, and asking for the address of the farm and a letter of introduction, I was soon on the way to the Château de Cossigny. To reach the château I had to cross a forest a mile long as night was setting in, and I did this, I remember, with my heart in my mouth, for boy-like I was timid when away from all human sound.

Never shall I forget that first night in my first situation, where, as a matter of fact, I was made to feel as much at home as I could be, being offered a seat at the supper-table in company with the farmer, his wife and two daughters, and the man who had charge of the stables. There was, indeed, such a lack of restraint about the entire proceedings, that I was emboldened to ask who played the different instruments I saw in the room (a flute, clarinette and violin), and the subject of music thus being touched upon, the evening ended in my playing several pieces on the violin, whilst the eldest girl contributed some French airs as her share of the evening's entertainment. If the previous night's bed had been hard and uncomfortable, what shall I say of my stable berth, which was the upper one, the lower and better one being occupied by the stable-man? In youth, however, one can rest almost anyhow and anywhere, and, as a matter of fact, I was still asleep in the morning when the stable-man aroused me and handed me a blouse, a pair of wooden shoes, and a drover's cap. Thus attired, I set forth on my duties, which consisted mainly in stable cleaning and taking the cows to grass. Farm life was so novel to me that I was in mortal dread of the poor beasts to begin with, but this fright wore off as I saw the stable-man pet them, by patting their fat necks and letting them lick his hands. I soon, in fact, grew too venturesome, for on attempting to ride a donkey that kept the cows company, this animal was butted by one of the cows and I had an ugly spill, which resulted in plenty of bruises for me.

Needless to say I refrained from further liberties with the frolicsome Fricotin, as the donkey was called. Supper-time and the sort of concert that followed made the days pass agreeably enough, especially as I ventured to ask for permission, which was readily granted me, to take the violin for practice into a hut in a corner of the park, where I used to sit and rest while the cows were grazing. I must have looked rather a ridiculous object with a shepherd's crook in one hand and a violin in the other, but I gave scant heed to such matters then, though thoughts of home and my mother often came to me in the midst of these rough surroundings. This very humble occupation was soon, thanks to the influence of M. de Cossigny, the lord of the manor, exchanged for something more congenial. Attracted, it appears, by my violin-playing, M. de Cossigny was led to make inquiries about me, which resulted in his questioning me upon several points himself, the upshot being that I was sent to fill the vacant post of junior clerk in the office of Maître Dulcori, the notary of Brie. This was promotion indeed, and I was not slow to appreciate it, especially as the notary's wife, who was many years her husband's junior, was very kind to me. But even this more creditable occupation was only short-lived, for a surprise awaited me one morning when I had been there but a few days. I was summoned from the office to the sitting-room, to find myself confronted with my father, who had come from Paris to fetch me home again. Sixty years ago travelling was not so easy as it is now, and, owing to my father's absence in the south of France, we had seen but little of him.

This meeting, however, called forth a deal of emotion on both sides, and it was some time before I was able to suppress my tears sufficiently to enable me to enter into the arrangements suggested by my father for our return to Paris by the diligence the next morning. On the journey I was sounded by my father as to my tastes and predilections, and when I unhesitatingly told him I had no vocation whatever for the priesthood (adding irreverently that I had been on my knees enough for one life-time), he, with the indulgence that was characteristic of him, replied, that he saw no reason why, music being my bent, I should not practise it, for a time, at all events, and await results. On nearing home I began to feel uneasy respecting the reception I should get from my mother, but once in the house, there was nothing to fear on this score, and the dinner proved a happy, peaceful time for us all. Nor did anything unpleasant occur for a long while to cloud the domestic horizon. Indeed, I was soon in high glee, for M. Ribard, a well-known music-master, and the conductor of some orchestral concerts given on Sundays at Choisy-le-Roy, was engaged to give me lessons on the violin. I was enrolled as violinist in the Choisy-le-Roy orchestra, a position I was proud to fill, seeing that I was but sixteen years of age. It happened that, about this time, the fortunes of the family were enhanced by the death of a rich uncle of my mother's, who left his money to be divided between his two nieces—my aunt Héloise and my mother. This sudden accession of wealth improved our position considerably, and every franc I had given to me by my father, or could coax out of my mother, I spent in attending good concerts, with an occasional theatre thrown in by way of variety.

I have already spoken of my mother's piety. Another of her characteristics was thrift, which is one common enough amongst middle-class provincial people in France, but in her case it may be said to have reached the point of miserliness, as the following little anecdote will show. I ought to mention that my mother, who was very fond of animals, kept what her friends called a singular trio, namely a small spaniel dog, a pretty gray angora cat, and a tiny Russian cock, and this happy family were almost inseparable, eating together, and playing and sleeping together, their bed being a large deep basket well lined, and comfortably padded with a loose cushion resting on a mass of odds and ends recruited from the bag of cuttings commonly used in families. Happening to cut my finger one day, I bethought me of the pets' basket for a piece of rag to bandage it with, and in rummaging over this my hand came in contact with something hard. This turned out to be a bag of five-franc pieces that had been hoarded and thus hidden by my mother. I remember to have had a box on the ear for making the discovery, besides being strictly enjoined never to divulge the secret to anyone—an injunction I obeyed, I need not say. On another occasion, when I went to a wardrobe in my mother's room, I came across an old sugar-basin full likewise of five franc pieces, but this time I took care to say nothing about it.

CHAPTER II.

Summer holidays—M. René Lafleur—The salle Montesquieu
—My first concert—Mdlle. Jeanne Loze—Auber and the
Tolbecque family—Le père Musard and Reicha—Musard
in London.

LIKE most youngsters of my age, I looked forward to the
summer holidays, which meant, in our family, six weeks
during the months of August and September being spent
in the country, the time being generally divided into a
fortnight passed with my grandmother at Nogent-sur-Seine,
a fortnight at Sens with my aunt Héloise, and a like period
in our own old village. They were happy times, though
they yielded little to which it would be worth while to draw
the attention of the reader. One incident, however, I will
take the liberty of narrating. Railway travelling was then
unknown, and we used as a rule to take the diligence which
went from Paris to Nogent in one night, a distance of thirty
miles. Sometimes we went by water, travelling by the
"coche," a large boat plying once a week with goods, and
having accommodation for a few cabin passengers, the journey occupying two days and two nights. A pleasant enough
method of travelling, when journeys are undertaken for
enjoyment. Nowadays, what preoccupies us most, is to
rattle over as many miles as we can in a given space of

time. The "coche" was towed along the bank by three
or four horses, and, on one occasion, I remember, when the
water was low, we stuck fast in the sands, and could move
no further. It was a lovely clear night, so there was no
panic, and as the skipper, if I may call him so, sent to a
neighbouring village for extra horses, there was nothing to
do but to wait patiently for the turn of events. But
even with four additional horses we still remained
embedded in the Seine, so there seemed no way out
of the difficulty but to land the passengers in the small
boats. The captain gave orders for this to be done, but it
proved such slow work, that, when one batch had been
landed another effort was made, and this time successfully,
to float the vessel, the passengers just landed joining in the
attempt by pulling at a rope attached to the mast.

Having arrived at Nogent in the morning, we were
collecting our traps and preparing to start for the Hôtel de
Jerusalem, when our dog, Sylvia, who always accompanied
us, was nowhere to be found. Search was made high and
low; my mother kept calling her pet, and I started whistling
for it, but no sign of the dog could be seen, and we
naturally began to fear the poor thing had been drowned in
the night, and therefore proceeded sadly on our journey
without it. It was Sylvia's shrill bark, however, that gave
us our first greeting as we drove into the courtyard of the
hotel. She had remembered our visit of the previous year,
and, after the manner of sagacious dogs, had gone on in
front as if to herald our approach.

But for the sad recollections recalled between my mother and grandmother of the destruction of the hotel already related in the opening pages of this volume, these holidays at Nogent would have been without a cloud. But the charred beams were there to tell the tale, for nobody had ever been able to induce the old lady either to leave the place or to have it restored. Still, they were restful and also happy visits, though they did not contain the element of mirth that pervaded my aunt's home at Sens, where the presence of two cousins, Armande and Auguste, who were very near my own age, gave an air of gaiety to the house only found associated with youth. From Sens, as I have said, we went to Aix-en-Othe to finish our holiday, and at the fête of the village, held on the first Sunday in September, there was a general meeting of the Rivière family. It mattered not that the music provided for the dancing, held on the lawn that faced the church, consisted of a scratchy violin and a squeaky clarinette. The young people tripped it merrily, and were as happy as if the best orchestra in the world had been engaged for their benefit. What delights belong to youth!

Returning to Paris in the autumn to resume my musical studies, I succeeded in composing a set of quadrilles that I called "La Fête du Roi." Thanks to the kindness of M. Ribard, who was conductor of one of the large open-air orchestras engaged by the city of Paris to perform on Louis Philippe's Fête Day, the 4th of May, my set of quadrilles was performed by his band of sixty musicians, and achieved a fair measure of success. A few years later " La Fête du Roi " was published by my old friend, René Lafleur, and it is still, I believe, in print. At the time I speak of, M. René Lafleur, who was considered the best violin bow maker in Paris, had a shop of quite modest appearance in the Rue du Petit-Pont near Nôtre Dame ; but, as his fame as a violin player and conductor increased, he removed to larger premises in the Rue des Petits Carreaux, and later again he migrated to the boulevards near the Porte St. Denis, where his business grew to such an extent that he made a large fortune, and was able then to indulge his bent, which was the cultivation of the artistic as well as the money-making side of the profession, terms that, as everybody knows, are not always synonymous. In this way, M. Lafleur organized an amateur orchestra society, of which I became the secretary. Practising took place in a concert-room called " La Salle de la Tête Noire," the conductor being M. Cornet. It was whilst I was engaged in this orchestra that I brought out my second composition, a set of waltzes, entitled " Héloise," after the name of an aunt, to whom I dedicated the piece, which was often played by the orchestra, and afterwards published by M. Lafleur. My advancement in the orchestra at this time became unexpectedly rapid, owing to the regrettable illness of M. Cornet, who, being obliged to give up his post as conductor, thought fit to name me as the most suitable member of the band to replace him, a position I held till conscription time came, when I was drafted into a regiment.

Another old concert-room I well remember as existing half a century ago, was that where the Duval Restaurant in the Rue Montesquieu now stands, which is, as many of my readers will know, near the Palais Royal and the Magasins du Louvre. At the time I write of, the orchestra of the Salle Montesquieu, as it was called, was conducted by an Italian named Bosisio, and it was here that the Philharmonic Orchestral Society gave their monthly concerts. The conductor of the Philharmonic concerts was M. Loiseau, who likewise filled the post of chef-d'orchestre at the Théâtre Français, a position soon after held by the renowned Jacques Offenbach. The Philharmonic orchestra, which numbered about eighty musicians, was composed chiefly of amateurs, who paid a monthly subscription, the leaders alone being remunerated for their services. Owing to the recommendation of my professor, I was admitted, from the first, without any subscription fee. And capital practice it was, for I was amongst the second violins for one season, and with the firsts afterwards. I grew then so familiar with the repertory of overtures, symphonies, and other orchestral works of this society, that I have never since needed a score for conducting them, as I have every movement committed to memory. The leading violinist was Charles Dancla, who is still, I believe, professor at the Conservatoire of Music in Paris.

About this time, that is to say, when I was eighteen years of age, my father, who had more ambition for me, I think, than I had for myself, determined to engage one of the

most noted violinists to give me finishing lessons, his choice
falling upon M. Marque, who was one of the principals in
the Musard concerts, then all the rage in Paris.   Under
M. Marque's tuition I attained sufficient proficiency to
justify M. Musard in selecting me to replace M. Marque
when this gentleman had private engagements to fulfil.
Better practice than this no young musician could have
had, and not to have profited by it would have denoted
ineptitude.   What with the interest taken in my pursuits by
both parents, and the support and sympathy that were
shown me in so many ways by my different masters, I was
encouraged, at this early age, to organize a concert.   For
this purpose I obtained the permission of our neighbour,
M. Loze, who was a veterinary surgeon, to use the large
space at the back of his house for my al fresco concert.
M. Lafleur kindly lent me the instruments and music-
stands used by our society, and quite a number of pro-
fessionals volunteered their assistance.   As a few more
brass instrument players were wanted, I applied to M.
Paul Brick, the brigadier-trumpeter of the 4th Hussars,
stationed at the Celestins barracks, to supply me with
these, and he at once promised to bring six or eight of his
colleagues with him to my concert.   Fine weather favoured
the entertainment, and a capital attendance was the result,
the programme containing, in addition to several well-
known   compositions,   Boildieu's   overture   "La   Dame
Blanche," and a new piece of my own, an overture, called
"Simple et Gracieuse."   The acquaintance thus begun

with Paul Brick, and which was I am sure conducive to happiness on both sides, lasted to the day of his death, in 1884. From trumpeter in the 4th Hussars, Paul Brick became bandmaster, and years after he was drafted into the Guides' celebrated band, which flourished under the Empire; subsequently, and on his retirement from active service, being appointed conductor of the Municipal Band at Cannes, a post he held till his death, which resulted from heart disease. I was indebted for a deal of the success at this my first concert, to the efforts made by Mdlle. Loze, the daughter of the veterinary surgeon above-named, to secure a good attendance. Her assistance and kindness were invaluable to me, and it was in gratitude for these friendly attentions of hers, that I dedicated my new composition "Simple et Gracieuse" to her, as a fitting tribute to her sweet appearance. Her untimely end, from suicide, brought about by her parents' refusal to allow her engagement to a young man because he had no means or position, was one of the biggest sorrows my life had till then known. The poor girl was romantic—stupidly so, perhaps; anyhow, when her father intimated to this particular admirer that he must cease his visits, for the prospect of their union did not suit him, she at once left home, and sent a note to say she should give nobody any further trouble. Her body was dragged out of the Seine a week after, and many were the tears shed over the grave of the sweet creature we had all unceasingly sought from the day of her departure.

D

It was a comrade as well as a friend I lost in Jeanne Loze, for we had been in the habit of practising together, on the piano and violin. After her death, which had a great effect upon me, feeling the necessity for some change in my mode of life, I resolved to leave the parental roof, and start a small home of my own, a proceeding I felt justified in adopting, as I was earning enough to satisfy all my modest requirements. Though far from rejoicing at this proposition, neither my mother nor father saw fit to oppose it, and I was soon installed in comfortable quarters at 21, Place Royale, near the Place de la Bastille, and two doors from where Victor Hugo then resided. My rooms, which were large and well furnished from my mother's stock, containing among other pet possessions the piano I made so little use of, commanded a nice view over a beautiful garden, and what with the relaxation from restraint that even the fondest mothers impose, often unwittingly enough I know, my new life became quite a pleasant one, especially as I found plenty of employment. Being a very good music copyist, I employed my leisure hours at this kind of work, and had often more on my hands than I could comfortably get through, whilst, by way of pastime, I took to rod-fishing, for the indulgence of which pleasure, not wanting to encroach upon my duties, I used to get up at daybreak. When engaged in this sport one morning, I had rather an unpleasant experience through changing, because the water looked clear and inviting, from rod to fly-fishing. Scarcely had I taken off my boots and left them together with a provision basket on the bank, in order to go into the river and have, as I thought, some really good sport, when a steamboat came along and so disturbed the water in its course as to send it up to my chin, besides carrying away my belongings from the bank before I could reach the shore to save them. My journey back to Paris, shoeless and soaked to the skin, was anything but a pleasant one.

It was at this early part of my career that I became acquainted with the Tolbecque family, and, as the mention of their name reminds me of Auber, and of his kindness towards them, I may as well here give the brief history of the early struggles of "The Tolbecque string quartett." These clever young brothers (they were four in number) were the children of poor parents, utterly without the means for educating them. Indeed, the boys, having natural musical talent, helped to support their parents by going into the streets to play and collect coppers. They chanced one day to play in Auber's garden, and the famous composer was so struck with their ability that he sent for them to be brought in to see him. On learning their history Auber magnanimously offered to obtain admission for them at the Conservatoire, and he helped them, at the same time, with money and in other ways. The Tolbecque brothers thus soon became great players, Jean Baptiste being, a few years after, and when Louis Philippe was on the throne, appointed conductor of the State concerts and balls at the Tuileries, composing during the time he held the position a deal of good dance music. The next brother, Jullien, was for many years conductor of the Variétés orchestra ; Auguste came to England, where he was leader at Her Majesty's opera under Costa, Balfe, and others during the Lumley management, and Isidor Tolbecque, who was a celebrated violincellist, and to whom I shall have occasion again to refer, became conductor, in turn, of several Paris theatres.

Recollections of le Père Musard, as he was popularly styled, also occur in connexion with the events of 1837. M. Musard was then conducting promenade concerts under an immense marquee in the champs Elysées, where, in fact, the Café des Ambassadeurs now stands. In addition to being a composer of light music Musard was a very sound musician. He had studied harmony at the Conservatoire in Paris, where he obtained the first prize in 1831, his professor being Reicha, the man to whom all musicians are indebted for the best Treatise on Harmony that has ever been published. This book is still in use at the Conservatoire.

Amongst Musard's compositions were a number of trios, quartettes, and quintets for stringed instruments that were highly thought of at the time, and it was soon after he obtained his first prize in the Harmony Class that he published his Nouvelle Méthode de Composition Musicale." This work, which he dedicated to his teacher, was in two volumes. The preface to the first volume runs thus :

A REICHA.

Toi qui fis briller le flambeau de la vérité dans un art qui, sans tes recherches, ne serait connu que d'un petit nombre, reçois, ici, le tribut de ma gratitude jointe à l'admiration la plus profonde de tes hautes connaissances. C'est avec crainte que j'ose aujourd'hui écrire sur une matière que toi seul, as su traiter. Initié par toi dans les secrets de cette science, il y a de la témérité à moi d'élever les regards jusqu'aux marches du trône où ton mérite a su te placer, mais elle peut être excusée, puisque tout l'honneur du bien que peut renfermer ce livre t'appartient.

Ton reconnaissant et dévoué élève,

P. MUSARD.

My library contains a copy of Musard's book, on the first page of which are the following lines written by Reicha :—

MON BON AMI,

Quelle surprise inattendue ne m'a-t'elle pas causé cette brochure que vous avez eu la bonté de me faire parvenir ; et combien je vous remercie pour le témoignage éclatant et public que vous rendez si franchement, si généreusement et si noblement à mes faibles talents. Vous dire que j'en suis on ne peu plus flatté serait inutile. Mais ce dont je suis le plus fier, c'est que vous avez si bien profité de mes conseils pour pouvoir, à votre tour, les transmettre aux autres ; et qui pourrait le faire mieux que vous ? Votre application, votre pénétration, votre philanthropie et votre bonne foi en sont garants ! Oui, je fais les vœux les plus sincères pour que votre enterprise soit couronnée de succès tel que vous le désirez, tel que vous le méritez à tous les égards.

Recevez, mon cher Musard, l'assurance de mon attachement, et de mon amitié inaltérables.

REICHA.

Musard, as I have already said, gave his concerts in the summer in the Champs Elysées ; and in the winter, with his orchestra, which was a large one, consisting of eighty musicians of undoubted talent, he migrated to the Salle Valentino, in the Rue St. Honoré, the Nouveau-Cirque of to-day. These concerts were popular for a number of years, and deservedly so, for Musard was a very able conductor, besides being also a prolific composer. He had not good looks to help him; indeed, his face was disfigured by the marks of small-pox, but there was an irresistible charm in his manner, that made him a most interesting man to talk to. Musard had a style, too, of his own in conducting. He was original, not to say eccentric, and this was shown even in his attire, for he wore his black evening coat buttoned almost up to the chin, which alone gave him a very singular appearance. I have said that his output of work was con-siderable; and whenever either a new set of valses, or a quadrille of his composition was performed, the audience was certain to be large. Except when I was replacing M. Marque as conductor, I used to spend my evenings at the Musard Concerts, and thus I became acquainted with most of the leading members of the orchestra. This included such well-known men as Bellon, who was the leader, the solo violins being Remy and Deloffre, whilst, still among the violins, were men like Dancla, Lelong, Leonard, and Amet. Then, there were Pillet and Seligmann, the violon-cellists; Durier and Loisel, the contre-basses; Bauller, who played the piccolo; Dorus, the flute; Dufresne and Forestier, the cornets; Dieppo, Simon, and Vobaron, the trombones, besides Pasdeloup, of concert fame, who played the kettledrum, and Auguste, the bass-drum player. There were many popular items, I remember, on the programme in those bygone days, but none more so than the duets for violin and violoncello, performed by Deloffre and Pillet. It was natural, of course, that Musard's fame in Paris should soon become the talk of musical London, and, as a consequence, it was not long before he was engaged by a firm of musical publishers for several seasons of similar concerts in the metropolis. It was whilst crossing the channel that Musard, who was not generally considered an impressionable man, made the acquaintance of a lovely Irish widow, who ultimately became Madame Musard.

CHAPTER III.

FROM Musard to the famous Jullien is but a step, and as the last-named was so popular for a series of years in England, I must claim my readers' indulgence for giving detailed reminiscences of him. I purpose depicting this world-famed man, exactly as he was when I first knew him. Jullien, who was the son of a bandmaster of the 32nd line regiment, played the piccolo in the band when a boy, and came to Paris with his regiment at about twenty-two years of age. He was also a good violin player. I have a vivid recollection of the first occasion on which I saw Jullien. He was conducting a modest orchestra of a dozen musicians at a ball at the Salon d'Apollon, situated at the Barrière Mont-Parnasse, and he was in the orchestra in his shirt-sleeves. The band used to play at that time a set of quadrilles composed by Jullien, and in which he had introduced a number of old French airs. "Rococo," for so the quadrille was called, was a great hit. This was in 1834, when gas light began to be used in Paris, and the proprietor of the Salon d'Apollon was one of the first to introduce the new light into his establishment. Jullien, who throughout his career aimed at novel effects, did not, of course, miss his chance of turning the gas to account, consequently he interpolated an old French air, "Il pleut bergère," into one of the figures of his Rococo quadrille, during which the gas was lowered, and leaves of brass tinsel imitating rain were showered upon the stage. So realism was not altogether unknown, even in the early thirties. Jullien's popularity grew fast, and at Carnival time he was engaged to conduct the orchestra at some half-dozen theatres for their Saturday *bals masqués*. In order to fulfil all these engagements he used to rush from one theatre to another in his cabriolet, which was easily recognizable, owing to the negro servant he had perched up behind, and thus he managed to conduct a quadrille at the Opéra Comique, and a valse at the Gaîté, Odéon, or elsewhere. Jullien seemed, in fact, to have the gift of ubiquity. At that time I was in the Gaîté orchestra as violinist, and I saw an immense deal of the popular conductor, who, however, in spite of his numerous and remunerative engagements, not only failed to amass wealth, but often left his musicians unpaid. I had good reason to know I was not the only member of his orchestra who had trouble with Jullien in this respect. He had moreover an amusingly lofty air with him, and when pressed for payment made a habit of referring the applicant to his "secretary," as if such mundane affairs as accounts were altogether beneath the notice of so great a man.   It was, I well remember, to his secretary that he referred my mother one day, when, on meeting him, she took the opportunity of reminding him that he owed me a matter of some fifty francs for arrears of salary.   As the result, probably, of my mother's complimentary reference to him as a "great musician," Jullien at once put his hand into his pocket and paid the overdue account.   My mother had unconsciously, and probably quite unintentionally, flattered his vanity, and this was one of the vulnerable points in Jullien's armour.   To the physiologist, Jullien would have been a most interesting study, for he was certainly a striking personality.   He was a perfect example of the mental unsoundness of genius, having peculiarities of manner which were more than mere eccentricities.

In 1838 Jullien was engaged for a series of concerts at the Jardin Turc on the Boulevard du Temple, a building that still exists.   He followed Jean Baptiste Tolbecque as musical conductor there, and I was engaged by Jullien as violinist for the entire season, the principal members of the orchestra being Remusat (flute), Lavigne (oboe), Le Cerf (clarionette), Beauman (bassoon), Paquis (horn), Messeurer (cornet), Dantonet (trombone), Prosper (ophicleide), and Artus (drums), some half-dozen of whom followed Jullien to London.   These concerts, I remember, created a great sensation.   They were the talk of Paris.   The price of

admission was but a franc, and the large garden was crowded
every night to its utmost limit, not to mention the hundreds
of people who flocked to the boulevard, remaining outside
to listen to the music, just as the promenaders do now in
the summer at the different open-air concerts in the
Champs Elysées. A certain sensation was created during
the season, first by the popularity of a new valse Espagnole,
entitled *Rosita*, and then by the dispute that took place
respecting the authorship of this composition. Some of
Jullien's enemies—for like most popular men he had
enemies—attributed this valse to one of Jullien's musicians,
an old Italian, named Philiberti, who, as a matter of fact,
had declared himself to be the composer of it. The affair
indeed led to an unseemly discussion, which was commenced by another member of the band, a fellow country-
man of Philiberti, named Capri, and in which Jullien
was struck in the face by Capri. The regulation duel
followed of course, but, to everyone's regret, Jullien came
off second best. In the minds of those competent to
judge, there was never any doubt as to the authorship of
Rosita, for it was in Jullien's distinctive style, resembling in
many respects his valse *Le Rossignol*, that was also a great
favourite, and in which Jullien, who was a magnificent
piccolo player, had introduced a solo for himself. There
was the orchestral score too (which was sold to the publisher
Troupenas) to show that *Rosita* was composed by Jullien.
If, however, I could personally have had any doubt in the
matter at the time, it would have been removed years later

by an experience of my own that occurred when I was in garrison at Lyons, in which city this same Philiberti was engaged at the Casino. The conductor of the orchestra there happened to be Charles Gourlier, an old friend of mine, so I had no difficulty in getting him to take up a set of waltzes I had composed, and that for some time held a place in the Casino programme. Great was my astonishment, however, on returning to Paris after spending seven years in the army, to find my waltzes published by Marguerita, in Philiberti's name. Upon remonstrating with him, the fellow coolly owned to the theft, alleging as an excuse, that he was hard up at the time, and so had appropriated my score and sold it for 2*l.*

Another incident in regard to Jullien, that occurred about the same period, is worthy of note. Meyerbeer's masterpiece, *Les Huguenots*, was new to Paris, where it had followed *Robert le Diable* at the Opéra, under the management of M. Véron, but it is no exaggeration to say the greatest stir made about this opera was due to Jullien, who, at the suggestion of Brandus, the publisher of the score, arranged a grand fantasia on *Les Huguenots*, introducing all the leading melodies, including the Lutherian Chant, La Bénédiction des Poignards, Le Massacre de la St. Barthélemy, and others. The finale, with its lime-coloured flames, produced an enormous sensation, the rolling of cannon and volleys of musketry being reproduced by the musicians with realistic and almost terrible effect. There was a reverse, however, to the medal, respecting this per-

formance. *Les Huguenots* being put last in the programme, came on the stroke of midnight, and remonstrances
became numerous from the inhabitants of the neighbourhood, who complained of having their slumbers disturbed by
this volume of music. Needless to say Jullien took no heed of
these complaints, till, one day, he received from the Com-
missaire de Police an injunction restraining him from continuing the performances of *Les Huguenots*. Jullien, who
was not a man to bow to authority, totally disregarded the
injunction, and went on with his selection, making, in fact,
the bombardment louder than ever—popularity at any price
being his motto. He had enormous bills posted all over
Paris, announcing that *Les Huguenots* would soon be replaced by a Grand Pastoral Fantaisie of his own composition. Read from a distance there was nothing remarkable
in the bills, but, printed in smaller type, between the big
lines, were some strictures on the police and the Government, couched in most indecorous language. This act of
bad taste on the part of the popular conductor met, as it
deserved to do, with speedy punishment, a warrant being
issued for his arrest. To escape the consequences of his
rash conduct, Jullien fled to London, and was condemned,
in his absence, to five years' imprisonment, or twenty
years' exile. He decided for the latter and remained in
England, where fortune continued to smile on him, much
as she had done in Paris.

Celebrated also, though in a different way, were Nourrit
and Duprez, two remarkable French tenors, who flourished

at the Grand Opéra in 1836, contemporaneously with
Grisi, Persiani, Rubini, Lablache, and Tamburini, who were
at the Italiens. Nourrit, who besides being a splendid
singer, was also a very fine actor, was chosen by the
management of the Grand Opéra to create the principal
rôles in *Guillaume Tell, Les Huguenots, La Juive, Masaniello*,
and other grand operas. Nourrit, in short, was the lion of
the hour, when, suddenly the musical world in Paris began
to get interested in a young tenor named Duprez, who had
made his *début* in Italy, and whose fame speedily spread all
over Europe. Duprez was at once engaged by the
manager of the Opéra, Rossini's *Guillaume Tell* being the
work chosen for the new tenor's first appearance. Nourrit
was so incensed at the engagement of Duprez, that he
tendered his resignation to the management, and set out
for Italy, accepting an offer to sing at San Carlo, in Naples,
a few days after the *début* of his rival in Paris. Duprez
had a wonderful reception, and speedily became more
popular than his predecessor, whereupon Nourrit's jealousy
increased to such an extent, that it ultimately turned to
madness, poor fellow. The French papers, as he read them
one after the other, were so loud in the praises of Duprez, that
Nourrit, not able any longer to restrain his rage, deliberately
went up to a top room of the hotel where he was staying,
and threw himself out of a window. He was killed on the
spot. Duprez, as it will be remembered, continued his
brilliant career at the Opéra where, as principal tenor, he
held undivided sway for more than twenty years. Ulti-

mately, on retiring from the stage, he opened a singing academy, in which institution he still teaches.

Happening about the same time as the events just related, was a catastrophe of a different nature, and from which, unhappily, results still more appalling ensued. I am referring to Fieschi's plot against the life of King Louis Philippe, whose assassination the notorious Italian anarchist planned to encompass on the occasion of a grand review held by the king of all the troops in garrison in Paris. To carry out his scheme, Fieschi hired a room on the fourth floor of a house that the king was to pass, facing the Boulevard du Temple ; and the infernal machine, a sort of mitrailleuse, was put in position close to the window where it would seem certain to strike the king. The explosion was heard all over Paris, and was the topic of general discussion till the wretch expiated his crime under the guillotine. The monarch escaped unhurt, but five officers of his escort, including General Danremont, were killed. The funeral of General Danremont and his brother officers, which took place at the Invalides, the mournful procession passing through Paris to the Père-la-Chaise, was a memorable sight for all who witnessed it.

Following shortly upon this, came an event in my career, which, though of importance to me, may be briefly passed over, conscription time being a period by no means prolific in incidents of general public interest to the reader. I confess to having seen the time approach with complacency, for I felt pretty certain of being declined for military service owing to my defective sight—an opinion, I may add, that was shared by my mother and the oculists we had, in turn, consulted on the matter. Consequently, it was without dismay in the year 1839 I saw the day for drawing the numbers approach. I drew the low number of three. When, however, a month later revision day arrived, and all the conscripts who had drawn low numbers were called up for examination before some half a dozen army surgeons (all specialists) a complete change came over me; for, after being examined, and hearing the question of my shortsightedness also discussed, I was astonished, as I retired to make way for another young fellow, to hear the ominous words, "Bon pour le service." I had not, and never had, I regret to say, the least military ardour in me, therefore the prospect of a soldier's life was one, I own, that inspired me with a feeling akin to terror. My parents were no less surprised than myself, and I well remember my mother, who was anything but a reckless woman with regard to general expenditure, making the suggestion of paying 200l. for a substitute for me; a proposition I refused to entertain for a moment, for I still held to the belief that, by appealing at the review to be held by the Inspector-General in eight or nine months' time, I should be released from further service. When however, it came to choosing a regiment, I decided for the infantry, stable work not being the least to my taste, to say nothing of the cowardly fear I had of being kicked by the horses, a feeling not uncommon, I believe, amongst civilians leading city lives. So, with a young friend named Bridou, I joined the 12th Regiment of light infantry in garrison at Verdun, near Metz, in order to be near Captain Jandier, a cousin of my mother's, who was in the same regiment. But for the companionship of Bridou I should have found that long diligence ride a very gloomy one, for railways were only beginning to be used then, and therefore were not general. In youth, however, one can make light of most things. It enabled us, for instance, to take no notice of the sneers of some of the commoner soldiers in the regiment ; the uneducated, rough, country fellows who delighted in jeering at our Paris-cut clothes, and what they called our " city ways." As to the uniform, I can recall the discomfort I felt on wearing the clumsy shoes, and the coarse, ill-fitting suit, with its five-inches stiff high collar, that was in use at the time, as well as if it were but yesterday. I am, moreover, conscious of having cut a very ridiculous figure as a soldier, the finishing touch to my appearance being given when a gun was handed to me for use in defence of my country. I did not feel a bit suited to my new rôle. Patriotism is a very fine feeling, but it is a relative term, and therefore a sentiment that we do not all feel in the same way.

Unluckily for me, when the time came for my appeal, Captain Jandier, upon whom I had relied to help me in this matter, had exchanged into a Zouave regiment bound for Africa, so I had to bear my lot with the best grace I could. Of course, I soon learnt how, by means of tips to

E

the sergeant or the corporal, to get into their good graces,
but with the drill-sergeant it was a harder matter, as, for
some reason, this man persisted in treating my short-
sightedness as if it were a sham, and, in consequence of the
mistakes I occasionally made, he reported me to the
captain.   Between the pair, therefore, I had not the happiest
time ; albeit, I resolved to obey all orders, and to keep my
temper beneath control, a matter at times somewhat difficult
of accomplishment.   For what was called clumsiness at gun-
practice I was humiliated by being sent to the kitchen as
assistant cook, where I was to be kept, so the captain gave
orders, till my sight got better.   This change of work
involved another variety of dress, and it was one that
certainly did not enhance my personal appearance.   No
more degrading garb, except, perhaps, that of a convict,
could be imagined ; nor were the duties, which consisted
of vegetable scraping and other menial labour that this new
position entailed, calculated to reconcile me to a soldier's life.
Still, I philosophized a bit, and in this way resigned myself to
my fate.   In spite, however, of scraping and peeling thousands
of carrots and turnips, I did not realize the captain's desire,
which would also, it is needless to say, have been my own, of
recovering from my short-sightedness.   Another unpleasant
incident connected with barrack life, was a punishment of
four days' arrest inflicted upon me for no other reason than
knocking a fly from my face that kept buzzing about me at
drill time one scorching afternoon.   This involuntary and
yet natural movement was called " moving in the ranks,"

and, as I have said, 'it was reported and punished as such.

By the advice of Captain de Castellane, who was an intimate friend of Captain Jandier, I took the necessary steps to be admitted into the band of the regiment, my object in not previously mentioning my knowledge of music having arisen from my desire to get out of the service altogether as soon as I could. Captain de Castellane was the band president, and the arrangements for my transference from the ranks to the band being speedily effected, life at the barracks henceforth became tolerable, and even pleasant. There being no longer any need to conceal my musical aptitudes, I wrote home for my violin, and in due time received, not my old instrument, that was worth but 3*l.*, but a fine violin by Lupot, who was one of the best Parisian violin makers, with a splendid silver-mounted bow made expressly for me by our old friend Lafleur. My good old father had thought to add still further to my delight by sending a substantial money enclosure, which I found, together with an affectionate letter, in one of the side pockets of the case.

To be a member of the band was one thing, but to play a wind instrument was quite another, and when the band-master, an Italian named Signor Conterno, asked me to choose between the bassoon and the French-horn, I naïvely replied that I had no choice, and was willing to try either. It was therefore decided, as the second bassoon would soon be finishing his time, that I should take his place, and Signor Conterno, who was a good clarinette and bassoon

player, undertook my instruction. The experiment proved
a failure. I could get no music out of the bassoon, and so
I turned to the French-horn, which, in those days, was an
instrument without valves, and played by moving the right
hand in the bell. Indeed, the cornet was the only valve
brass instrument, and this had but two pistons—very
different from those in use now. The French-horn seemed
to suit me very well, and after a month's practice I managed
to play a good part, for which I received extra payment.
I found it an easy matter, also, to obtain permission to
exchange the barracks for private apartments, and this
enabled me to continue my studies on the violin, which,
however, I had to do without tuition, there being nobody in
Verdun with as much knowledge of this instrument as
myself. Being also allowed to wear civilian dress after
the hours of military duty, and to take my meals with the
non-commissioned officers instead of with the rank and
file, there was nothing much at this point of my career left
to complain of.

My knowledge of music also procured me the pleasure of the acquaintance of the colonel commanding
the regiment, which ended in my becoming a constant
visitor at Colonel de Pourailly's house, where I played violin
accompaniments for his wife, who was a charming blonde
of extreme affability, besides being a very good pianist.
Indeed, time in this way passed so agreeably, that, when
the general inspection was held, I forgot all about my
appeal for relief from service, and retained my position in

the band, spectacles and all. Either from love of change, however, or from a desire to take a more prominent position in the band, I soon arranged to give up the French-horn, in which, moreover, I knew I could easily be replaced, and to turn my attention to the alto-ophicleide. And it so happened that, although we had eight bass-ophicleides in B flat in the band, there was not one alto in E flat, albeit an important part for this instrument was published in all the current musical journals, and the instrument itself, which was a good one with twelve keys, made by Muller, of Lyons, formed part of the band property. After a little practice, I attained what was spoken of at the time as remarkable proficiency on the ophicleide, and in this way my popularity with the officers of the regiment increased.

Still, the life at Verdun, that had begun so disagreeably, also ended sadly, for I was an eye-witness of the execution of a young trombone player belonging to a regiment of dragoons, who, for having struck the bandmaster with his trombone, was tried by court-martial, and condemned to be shot. A deal of sympathy was expressed for the young fellow, who, had been punished by the bandmaster, a German, for an imperfect rendering of a certain passage on his trombone, the punishment inflicted having been two days' confinement. This unjust and tyrannical treatment led the trombone player to commit the offence, for which he suffered death in presence of all the troops of the garrison, the different regiments being drawn up in a large square on the Place d'Armes, in front of the citadel, twelve soldiers firing at the word of command, and sending their comrade into eternity. The preliminary was first gone through of the sentence being read over to him, and the buttons torn off his coat. I shall not forget the scene. It was a very sad one.

In the summer of 1841, after a sojourn of two years at Verdun, the regiment was ordered to the camp at Chalons. Recollections of this place recall what seemed to me, and also to my companions of the time, to be an extraordinary stroke of luck I had whilst playing billiards at a place called St. Menehould ; the remarkable circumstance being that I was a comparative novice at the game, for I was not, and never have been billiard player, and yet I won three pools of 15 francs each in succession, much to the chagrin of the other players, some of whom, I believe, were half inclined to suspect me of unfair dealing. I had been thoughtlessly playing with rather a rough lot of men, an experience, I need hardly say, that I avoided in future.

On reaching Chalons, after walking from twenty-five to thirty miles a day, we had to live under canvas for four months, which, to the born civilian, is anything but an ideal existence. However, the country round being pic-turesque, and the weather lovely, excursions in the neigh-bourhood made the time pass pleasantly enough. I was also still engrossed with the ophicleide, for proficiency in playing which I was soon promoted to be corporal in the band. Only about two-thirds of the fifty musicians com-posing the band belonged to the band proper, the remainder were civilians specially engaged, and well paid to play the solo parts. These civilians, I remember, were mostly foreigners, Germans and Italians predominating. Strange to say, I never came across a British subject serving thus in the French army. Amongst the compositions that engaged my leisure hours at this period were several marches that became popular in the regiment, one, in particular, for the full reed band with the addition of bugles and drums, being considered original and effective by the officers, with whom I was fast becoming a favourite.

It was whilst at Chalons that I took some of the longest walks of my life, and here it was also that my appetite assumed the dimensions known only to youth. I have a vivid recollection of one meal in particular that my young friend Bridou and myself ordered, and enjoyed, at a restaurant on the banks of the Marne, and the *pièce de résistance* of which was a fat goose that we demolished entirely. This sounds like gluttony, which of course it was, but the digestion of youth is a remarkable thing. However, as for centuries it has baffled the theories of the medical profession, it is needless for me to attempt to solve any of these mysteries of Nature. I should only hopelessly fail.

The regiment was ordered in the autumn to take garrison at Lyons, a journey that entailed a twenty days' march, with an occasional rest of twenty-four hours in towns like Troyes, Dijon, and Macon. During this march through the Burgundy district, I remember we passed the gates of

the celebrated Clos-Vougeot, which is considered by most
people to be the best Burgundy vintage in France.   In
accordance with an ancient custom, the regiment in passing
in front of the distillery paid military honours.   The inmates
did not, however, return the compliment of our music by
offering us a taste of their wine.   After a spell of marching
through bad, stormy weather, we ultimately reached the
city of Lyons, and I had no sooner secured for myself
furnished apartments than I turned my attention once more
to my musical studies, and becoming acquainted with
George Haine, who was conductor of the Opera House
there, I was engaged amongst the violins in the orchestra
for the winter season.   It was whilst I was fulfilling this
engagement that Donizetti's opera *La Favorite* was performed for the first time in Lyons.   What an impression this
music created, to be sure!   The Wagnerian school was
practically unknown then, and Rossini, Meyerbeer, Halévy,
Auber, Donizetti, and others, were attracting and satisfying
the millions.

CHAPTER IV.

GARRISON life was relieved in the spring of 1842 by the arrival in Lyons of le père Musard, who was engaged to conduct four grand orchestral concerts, and with whom I was very naturally delighted to renew acquaintance. The pleasure of the meeting was, I am sure, mutual, if for no other reason than that Musard, being a stranger to the city, was glad to get me to be his guide for a time. I had a place as violinist in his orchestra, and I undertook to look after his music for him. Enormous preparations were made for these concerts, and amongst the many prominent names on the posters, was that of the well-known cornet player, M. Dufresne, who was considered a wonder. It so happened, however, that the brothers Joseph and Cesar Luigini, two remarkable cornet players, were fulfilling an engagement at the Lyons Opera House, and when Dufresne heard their performance, and realized that he could not compare favourably with them, he pretended illness, and returned to Paris ostensibly for medical advice. What seemed to be an almost insurmountable difficulty in the way of the proper execution of a grand selection from Meyerbeer's *Huguenots* at these concerts was overcome, I remember, through my intercession, a small matter for which Musard was immensely grateful, as he had reckoned upon having great success with his selection. At rehearsal everything went well enough till the trombone solo in the romance *Plus blanche que la blanche Hermine* came to be played, when it was found that none of the three players could manage it, the first trombone player having an in-strument in F alto, the second a B tenor, and the third a G bass. The piece was about to be discarded altogether by Musard, when I suddenly bethought me of a young Breton named Puchot in the 29th Regiment of the line, who had recently taken the First Prize at the Paris Con-servatoire, and was a magnificent performer. It was the work of a very few hours for Puchot to be interviewed by Musard and engaged for the four concerts. In ratification of a promise then made in Lyons, Puchot, years after, became a member of Musard's orchestra in Paris, and for some time he was one of the nine trombone players at the Opera balls.

I have already said that it was ambition which led me to learn the alto ophicleide, but it was chance, and chance only that was responsible for my studying the bass drum.

On a very slippery day in winter the man who was playing
this instrument fell and broke his leg, the accident keeping
him for three months in the hospital. The bandmaster,
Signor Conterno, made a dozen or more of the men try,
but, one after the other, they all failed. Even the principals in the band broke down. In a rash moment I
offered to fill up the breach, when the bandmaster, in quite
sympathetic tones, assured me it would not have occurred
to him to ask a " little Parisian " like myself to tackle such
a formidable instrument. I was inclined afterwards to
regret my impulsive offer, for, during three long months I
had to walk at the head of the band, playing *pianos*, *cres-
cendos*, and *fortes* on the bass drum alternately in marches,
overtures, and operatic selections. It was probably owing
to the aptitude I had for quickly learning a good many
instruments that I obtained one or two rapid advances at
different times in my career. One of these unexpected pro-
motions came about this period, just when in 1843 the War
Minister issued a decree expelling all foreigners from
band work in the French army. In pursuance of this
order our bandmaster, Signor Conterno, had to resign his
post, and no suitable substitute for him being found amongst
the pupils of the military school, an establishment existing
in Paris at that time under the title of the *Gymnase Musical*,
for the purpose of training young bandsmen for the post of
bandmaster, I had the temerity to apply for the appointment, which, with the aid of the band president, in addition
to a kind word put in for me by the Colonel's wife, I suc-

ceeded in obtaining. I was able, after this, to forget the resentment I had felt at being sent into the kitchen to scrape carrots and peel potatoes.

I was spurred on to fresh efforts in my new position, for it was my intention to retain it, and also to be on good terms with the officers of the regiment. Nothing, therefore, that perseverance or punctuality could accomplish was neglected by me, and as I wore the same uniform as the officers, and took my meals with them, and was, moreover, remarkably well paid, besides having leisure enough to fulfil an engagement as violinist at the Opera House, I soon grew to think that even a soldier's life could have charms about it.

It was while in garrison at Lyons that I made the acquaintance of the Arban brothers, who, in their different ways, were all remarkable men. Louis, the eldest, was the aeronaut of the day, and his ascents in 1842-43 created quite a sensation, till, like most balloonists, he went up never to be heard of again. This fatal ascent took place from a square in Madrid. The second brother, Charles, was proprietor of a grand casino in Lyons, called "La Rotonde," where concerts and balls were held all the year round. In addition to this onerous occupation Charles Arban managed to superintend a large manufactory of fireworks bearing his name, besides also finding time for certain ingenious inventions, one of which was a flying machine, that however, if I remember rightly, went no higher than the chimmey pots when the experiment was tried in the gardens of La Rotonde. The lion's share of ability, however, in the Arban family fell to Jean Baptiste, who developed talent at a very early age, and became at once a remarkable performer on the cornet-à-pistons. I well remember Jean Baptiste Arban's appointment as cornet solo in the picked band that went out to St. Hélène on board the *Belle-Poule*, under the command of the Prince de Joinville, to bring back the remains of Napoleon I. for sepulture in the Invalides. This clever cornet player was also a particularly affable man, and instances of his good nature were constantly occurring. One that came within my own experience is worthy of passing mention, for it happened on the first day of our acquaintance, when no laws, written or unwritten, could have called for the gracious concession he made to play a cornet solo at a concert I was giving on a summer afternoon at the Salle St. Barbe. Arban, who was in his sailor's dress had neither cornet nor music with him, but I had no sooner made the suggestion for him to oblige us with something than he was ready to mount the platform with an instrument borrowed from the band, and to play the "Carnaval de Venise" with variations, which he did in marvellous style. Our friendship, which was sealed from that day, lasted for nearly half a century, till, in fact, the day of his death in 1889. Arban was always acknowledged to be one of the best cornet players in France. This was clearly the opinion of Jullien, who engaged him in conjunction with Kœnig, as the two soloists in his orchestra, when he was in the zenith of his popularity in London. Kœnig excelled in slow movements, but when what is called tonguing was wanted Arban had no equal. On his return to Paris he was appointed professor of the cornet class at the Conservatoire, a post he held till his death. Besides being a very fine player, Arban was also a composer of some note, his musical achievements consisting of cornet solos, studies, etc.; whilst to him the musical world is indebted for a book called Arban's " Cornet Tutor," which is still considered the best that has ever been published. As conductor also of the Paris Bals de l'Opéra Arban will long be remembered, for this is a post he filled for years, till in fact the winter of 1889, when he caught the chill which killed him. Arban, who had never been an extravagant man, amassed a comfortable fortune, which on his death went to his only daughter. Many were the projects he formed as we used to sit chatting together, of ending his days on the shores of the Mediterranean we both loved so well. And with this object in view he bought land enough to build two villas upon in Monte Carlo, occupying his leisure in superintending the construction of the houses ; but, as I have said, he died in harness in the capital.

It was also when with my regiment in Lyons that I made the acquaintance of another noted musical family. I refer to Signor Luigini and his three sons, Joseph, César and Alexandre.   The father for many years had been solo trumpet player at the Opera House, at the time when valvè instruments being unknown, the slide trumpet alone was in use. As soon as the cornet-à-pistons was invented the sons took up the new instrument, at which they became experts ; but Joseph was soon called upon to succeed to his father's position at the Opera, whilst the second post was given to César, and Alexandre, who was then very young, played the triangle in the orchestra. Joseph Luigini soon gave up playing for conducting, and for years he wielded the bâton in the orchestra of the Lyons Opera House. César Luigini, wanting to see the world, accepted a brilliant engagement as solo cornet at the Lisbon Opera, where he died soon after, and Alexandre then stepped into his brother's shoes, and from cornet player was soon appointed bandmaster of the Municipal band at Tarare, a manufacturing town not far from Lyons, where he still resides. And yet Alexandre Luigini failed, some years later, to please Londoners during an engagement under Jullien, junior, for a series of promenade concerts at Her Majesty's Theatre. Coming after Arban and Kœnig, who had been great favourites, Luigini, whose style was different, evoked no enthusiasm whatever. A similar result occurred, I remember, in the case of Delpech, the cornet soloist from the Monte Carlo concerts. Joseph Luigini was succeeded in his post of conductor of the Lyons Opera by his son, who is still there, and is moreover considered one of the best conductors in France. My musical library contains a number of Luigini's compositions, including his Egyptian and Russian ballets, which, with others of his pieces, often figure in my programmes. It was after leaving Luigini one day at the Opera, where we had been rehearsing, that I had a narrow escape from a terrible omnibus accident, which resulted in the death of several of my fellow-passengers. It was blowing a terrific gale at the time, and thinking to escape the force of the hurricane I took the omnibus following the banks of the Rhône in the direction of Perrache, where I lived. Suddenly a cyclone overturned the vehicle. With three other passengers I managed to escape, and together we clung to a tree, but we were horrified to see the omnibus carried along several yards by the force of the wind, after which it rolled down the embankment into the Rhône, where horses and passengers were drowned. The forces of nature are not only beyond man's control but also beyond his comprehension. Thankful though I was at my own merciful escape on this occasion, a terrible sense of helplessness depressed me and my companions as we saw our unhappy fellow-passengers hurled to their doom without being able to put out a hand to save them.

A fearful gale was raging too, I remember, when my regiment started from Lyons to Nîmes, and we had about twenty consecutive days' marching. The currents we had to cross were so swollen that, on one occasion, the water being above our waists, we had to retrace our steps and seek shelter in a village, where we were billeted in two's and three's on the quiet inhabitants. In other respects the change was an agreeable one, there being a picturesqueness and a charm, all its own, in this route which shows such a thorough change of vegetation.

There is no need for me to describe a well-known town like Nîmes. Many of my readers will have seen for themselves the curious Roman ruins it contains, including the Temple of Diana, the Maison Carrée, La tour Magne, the Arenas, and the celebrated Roman baths with their fountains. With an eye to business always, as soon as we were comfortably installed in our new quarters, I set about finding an evening engagement, and I was not long in obtaining the post of first violin at the Grand Théâtre, where an opera company was performing, with M. Broukere, a Belgian, as *chef-d'orchestre*. At the same desk with me was young Calabresi, who afterwards become conductor of the Opera at New Orleans (U.S.A.), and who was subsequently appointed director of the Monnaie Theatre in Brussels, where he still is. Strange to say, the Nîmes *prima donna* was an Englishwoman, named Cundell; the possessor of a magnificent mezzo-soprano voice, and an excellent actress to boot. Miss Cundell, whom I met again in London some thirty or more years later, took the town of Nîmes by storm at the time I am speaking of by her singing of the rôle of Catarina in Halévy's *Reine de Chypre*. The leading tenor was Duluc, who had started life at Toulouse, as his parents had done before him, in the honest but humble calling of butcher, when somebody discovered that he had a fine tenor voice, and advised him to study music at the Toulouse Conservatoire. There is nothing of my experiences at Nîmes worth recording, for what I remember principally of the town was the bull-fights

F

that I considered a sickening spectacle, and on which I invariably turned my back when conducting my band at the performances. I remember the mosquitoes, too, for they made my life a torture. There is evidently a deal in the association of ideas, for whenever the city of Nîmes is mentioned in my presence my mind instinctively recalls bull-fights and mosquitoes, to the exclusion, I am bound to own, of all the lovely Roman ruins the place contains.

From Nîmes the regiment went to Cette, a mercantile sea-port town on the shores of the Mediterranean, where mosquitoes flourished more abundantly even than at Nîmes. We reached the town in winter in the midst of a gale, and saw some thirty vessels of different nations trying to enter the port. Seven of them, however, were completely wrecked, and another, a Dutch vessel, was carried by an immense wave and thrown, or, rather pitched, upon the sands, where it remained for a twelvemonth before it could be floated again. There was not such scope at Cette for me to push myself forward in the musical world, for the town only boasted of a third-rate theatre, but, as neither the billiard-room nor the canteen ever offered any attraction for me, in order not to waste my evenings, I accepted an engagement in the orchestra of the theatre, and as I soon made the acquaintance of the *greffier* of the Tribunal of Commerce, a M. de Pleuc, and his family, all of whom were musical, the daughters being good pianists, and the father a very clever clarinette player, I had no occasion to regret this further change of quarters. I called a polka that I composed about this time Sidonie, after Mdlle. de Pleuc, dedicating it to her father, to whom I was not a little indebted for countless acts of kindness and hospitality. Before long I got to know all the musical people of the town, and as I joined their philharmonic society, we were able, with the assistance of a few of my bandsmen, to organize some capital concerts. In the summer I gave them on the water, just in front of the colonel's residence, the platform on which we performed consisting of three or four barges fastened together, each being decorated with Venetian lanterns and tricolor flags. The scene was a gay one, and the concerts were a great success. Poor M. de Pleuc was killed some time after this in a railway accident, and among the many friends who regretted his premature end, none, probably, had more reason for mourning him than myself. Disinterested affection is not common, and when death takes from us those who have lavished it upon us the wrench is a painful one.

An unpleasant incident that involved the sacrifice of my liberty occurred during my sojourn at Cette. Living on the mountain-side of the town, in one of the " baraquettes," or villas, was a gentleman who gave himself the sobriquet of Napoleon. On the occasion of his birthday this individual applied to me to supply him with a band of some fifteen men for the entertainment of his guests. The evening was a success all round, a good dinner, good company, and, what was generally admitted to be good music. When the hour for breaking-up came, our host determined to see us back to the town. Probably some of his guests wanted a little looking after, but certain it is that I ought to have remembered, when he asked me to let my band strike up a lively tune, that it was against the rules of the regiment for the band to play in the streets out of regulation hours. Possessed, as I always have been, with the spirit of discipline, I have never, to this day, understood how I came to forget the rule, but as I had to pay for my imprudence by a week's imprisonment, the circumstance made a lasting impression upon me. When appealed to by the commanding officer to explain the freak, I could, of course, do nothing but apologize. Military discipline having, however, to be observed, I was sent to prison for a week. The confinement within the narrow limits of a cell was anything but pleasant; still I got a certain amount of amusement out of reading the prose remarks and the verses of poetry, some witty, some ribald, and some sentimental, with which my predecessors in captivity had adorned the walls. Having, luckily for me, a friend in the adjudant, I was supplied with books and writing materials, and also with more bed covering. I was even in sufficiently good spirits to indulge in some practical joking with comrades passing under my window when I could do so without being observed. During my incarceration the general inspection of the regiment was made by General Feucheres, and as I had known him at Nimes, when he entered my cell and recognized me, after inquiring the nature of my offence, he tapped me on the shoulder, and said, "Go out on duty again." Needless to say I did not want telling twice, but was soon in the central yard of the barracks, conducting my band, and having, as a matter of fact, suffered nothing but the loss of a little dignity from the three days' seclusion I had undergone. After this matters went on smoothly enough for a time, and just as I was getting used to my residence at Cette, an order came from the War Office for the 12th Regiment of Light Infantry to be ready to sail for Africa in a month. This did not fall in with my views in the least, for though desirous, as a rule, of seeing new places, my term of service having only another year to run, I did not relish the thought of being sent as far as Africa. To circumvent the authorities therefore, I devised the mean expedient of pretending illness, and in this I was assisted by a young Parisian friend, a medical student, named Philippe, who happened at the time to be assisting the surgeon of our infirmary. All that I had to do was to manage to look too low and weak to undertake a sea voyage, and with the aid of a clay pipe full of strong tobacco (smoking being a habit I had not then, nor have since, acquired), this was no difficult matter. The trick, which I have already owned to as a very mean one, succeeded so well that, upon being visited by the head doctor, I was, owing to my deplorable appearance, ordered at once to the hospital, where I remained under the care of Sister Marceline until the vessel conveying the troops had left for Algiers. I do not think Sister Marceline was taken in by my shamming, but she was kind enough never to betray

me, and in return for this consideration I did what I could
in helping her during the night watches with the sick and
dying patients. It was, therefore, anything but a lively
fortnight I passed in the hospital, but I was delighted to
be able to finish my time in France. The band having
accompanied the regiment to Africa, and only a depôt-
battalion being left at Cette, I had to seek the advice
of Major Breton, the officer in command, as to what
position I could now take up, and in the end it was
decided that I was to do what I could to form a fresh
band. With the assistance of the few bandsmen who had
been left behind, and a little training on my part of some
recruits, this was easily managed. I took to the slide
trombone myself in the place of the alto ophicleide, this
instrument having gone with the band to Africa, and in
three months we had quite a respectable band. I soon
became on friendly terms with Major Breton, and as his
wife and daughter were very musical my social pleasures
left nothing to be desired. This family took a deal of
interest also in the singing classes I organized amongst the
soldiers, and which were held three times a week. The
regiment was being supplied with musical instruments from
Besson, the celebrated brass instrument maker of Paris,
and when I wrote and asked him to let me have a good
tenor slide trombone, for my personal use, at as low a rate
as he could charge me, I was surprised at receiving a superb
electro-plated instrument with my initials engraved on the
bell, together with a most flattering letter, begging my

acceptance of the instrument. This trombone, which, apart from the fact of its being a beautiful instrument, I valued for sentimental reasons, was, I regret to say, lost during the riots in Paris in 1848. I was then a member of H. Marx's orchestra at the Château Rouge, and was in the habit of leaving my instrument in the band-room. It happened that a regiment of dragoons took possession of the establishment during the Revolution, and, presumably, when they went away my trombone travelled with them. Anyhow, I never saw it again, and, strange to say, I have never since chanced to play a note on the trombone.

As the time drew near for my discharge from the army I began to feel sorry at having to part from Major Breton, the more so as he was good enough to express a deal of regret at losing me. He was soon after appointed colonel, and was subsequently made a general. I had but few opportunities of meeting Major Breton after I left the army, but it was a grief to me, in 1856, to see his name amongst the list of killed at the battle of Malakoff, during the Crimean War.

CHAPTER V.

THOUGH parting with my military companions was, when the time came, something of a trial, the return to Paris, and the reception given me by my parents, gave somehow an added charm to existence, and one it would be difficult for me to describe. A seven years' absence from home in youth is a long one, and a considerable change had, of course, taken place in my appearance, and this was the more noticeable owing to the military uniform I was wearing when my father and mother came to meet me, and to conduct me to their new home in the Rue des Boulangers in the Faubourg St. Germain. The house, of which they were the only occupants, was comfortable in the extreme, and my room, which had been most cosily arranged by my mother, presented quite an inviting aspect, for the dear, thoughtful soul had hoped to give me pleasure by putting my old piano in this apartment. As a matter of fact I had given up pianoforte playing during my military service, consequently, except that the instrument helped to adorn the room, it had no *raison d'être* there.

I had not been at home many days before my mother introduced the subject she had long been cherishing, and had more than once referred to in recent letters, of my marriage. Such of my readers as understand the system of early marriages abroad, arranged by the respective families of the contracting parties, rather than by the young people themselves, will not need to be told by me that this is one of the things they do not manage better in France. Having had experience of marriage both in France and England, I can claim to speak *en connaissance de cause,* and it is without hesitation I express myself in favour of the English custom of courtship. Dickens, I know, makes one of his characters (it is Mrs. Nickleby, I think) declare in this connection that it is best to begin with a little aversion, but I am not inclined to endorse this view. Like the conventional son, therefore, of conventional parents, I allowed myself to be introduced in the conventional way to a family of well-to-do commercial people owning a marriageable daughter they wanted to see settled in life. From the first, I was not struck with M. Zink, my prospective father-in-law, who was an Alsatian in a large manufacturing business in the enamel earthenware stove line. · Nor, truth to tell, was I much fascinated by the pretty face and ample accomplishments of the daughter Caroline, but this lack of enthusiasm on my part arose, I thought at the time, from my preference for blondes, whereas Caroline Zink was a pronounced brunette.   And yet, albeit I had not any marked predilection for marriage, and felt, as I have said, no irresistible affection for my *fiancée*, more to avoid thwarting my parents than anything else, I drifted, as many a young man has done before me, into marriage with a girl of whose nature and disposition I knew absolutely nothing. When, however, the nuptial knot was tied, there was a firm determination on my part at all events to make a success of the speculation (for, if the term lottery is applicable to English unions, it is still more so to those contracted in France) and such, for a time, it seemed to be.   But I was doomed later, and from no fault of my own, to suffer man's greatest wrong.   I drained the cup of misery to its dregs. The blow was almost as great a one to my parents as myself, for they felt that but for them this marriage with a frivolous woman would never have taken place.

Let me dismiss this sad subject, however, and return to my musical career.   In partnership with Isidore Tolbecque, my own small capital not sufficing for such an enterprise, I took the Salle Bonne Nouvelle, on the boulevard of that name (on the spot where the Magasin of La Managère now stands) for a series of concerts and masked balls.   We engaged the best talent we could for the orchestra, which included Arban and Boulcourt as cornet soloists, Boulcourt years after being solo cornet player at the Argyll Rooms in London under Laurent and Lamotte.   We naturally looked forward to reaping a fine harvest during carnival time, but the Revolution of February, 1848, led to Louis-Philippe's Government being replaced by a Republic, and business of all kinds was brought to a standstill.   We had, consequently, to abandon our scheme of balls and concerts, and after paying all contracts, which our capital just enabled us to do, I found myself penniless, and at the same time considerably discouraged at having to begin the world afresh.

On my return to Paris, after leaving the army, I naturally looked up some old friends, one of my first visits being for le père Musard, who was good enough to express great delight at seeing me again.   I was struck by the change in his appearance.   The gout, from which he was a terrible sufferer, had aged him considerably, and he looked, and was a broken-down old man.   Despite the fact, however, that he had made a large fortune, instead of living quietly in his handsome villa at Auteuil, where he was mayor of the town and much respected, Musard persisted in coming to Paris to conduct the masquerade balls at the Opera, though, owing to the gout, he was unable to stand on his legs, which were encased in high furred boots reaching above the knees.   I was present at the last ball conducted by Musard, and I shall never forget the scene.   It was the custom in those days for the conductor, if a popular man, to be carried round the building in triumph, and Musard had always submitted to the process.   Jullien and myself later had the same doubtful honour conferred on us, for protestation was of no avail. But on the occasion now referred to, poor Musard felt unequal to the ordeal, and this was explained to the dozen

men who came to the front of the orchestra to take possession
of him.   All to no purpose !   Argument was unheeded, and
the tottering old conductor was dragged from the platform
and hoisted on to the shoulders of a stalwart Pierrot, the
procession taking its usual course round the opera house
and the *foyer*, the crowd following and shouting " Vive
Musard !   Vive Musard ! "   Masquerading of this kind
when practised on a young man was well enough, but it was
more than the fast-waning powers of the veteran conductor
could endure, and when I saw one of the processionists as
they were nearing the orchestra, put his heavy brass helmet
with a bang on to Musard's head, it seemed to me as if the
last flicker of his life must die out.   As a matter of fact he fell
back exhausted in the orchestra, from which he was quietly
borne, not in triumph this time, but by friends who in sorrow
gently put him into his carriage, which he was destined never
to use again at the opera.   The poor old conductor lingered
on for some years, and a terrible impression was made
upon my mind the last time I visited him at Auteuil
with some friends.   He was sitting on a wooden seat in
the garden all alone, bent double with infirmity, and with a
vacant look in his face that too plainly betrayed the loss of
his reason.   To those of us who had known Musard well
the news of his death came at last as a relief rather than a
sorrow.   The large fortune amassed by the famous conductor
was inherited by his son, Alfred Musard.

During my lesseeship of the Salle Bonne Nouvelle, I
made the acquaintance of one of the leading music pub-

lishers in Paris, M. Bernard-Latte, whose place of business was on the Boulevard des Italiens at the corner of the Passage de l'Opéra.   In the afternoon his shop was the rendezvous of all the leading musicians and journalists of the day.   Here in turn, I met Auber, Rossini, Meyerbeer, Donizetti, Adam, Halévy, and Fiorentino among others, all of whom were intimate friends of Bernard-Latte the publisher of *Norma*, *Lucia*, *La Favorite*, and scores of other popular operas.   Bernard-Latte and myself were soon very fast friends, and when he became lessee of the residence of the Duc de Padoue in the Rue de la Chaussée d'Antin, and transformed the place into a splendid hall and garden, which he called the "Casino Paganini," it was to me he applied to conduct the orchestra for him, a position I was only too glad to accept, having regard to my recent money losses.   At once I set about engaging a good orchestra of forty musicians, among the principals being Chevalier (violin), Bousquet (flageolet), Genin (flute), Selmer (clarinette), Lemonier (horn), Schlotmann (cornet), Rome and Richir (trombones), and Richard (ophicleide), all noted performers.   The new Casino proved a great success, and its prosperity continued till the ground was bought by the company of the Chemin de Fer d'Orléans, and converted by them into their central office.   It was during this engagement that I became one of the original members of the Society of Composers of Music, and from which, by right of seniority, I receive an annual pension.

When the exhibition of 1855 was held, I obtained, for

the firm of which M. Zink was the head, a good space in the building with a view to carry out an idea that I thought might succeed. My plan was to have an immense chimney-piece constructed of black marble. This was handsomely sculptured, and ornamented with three very large panels of white enamel earthenware ; and, as the Crimean war was at its height, it occurred to me to have the panels representing Turkey, France, and England, painted by one of the first artists in Paris. This was very successfully carried out, the chimney-piece was awarded a first-class medal, and was bought with its three panels by the Government for one of the rooms of the Ministry of War, where I believe it still is.

Compelled to move from the Casino Paganini, owing, as I have said, to the expiration of the lease, M. Bernard-Latte transferred his orchestra to another large concert hall. This building, which was called the Salle Ste. Cecile, was also in the Chaussée d'Antin. The entertainment was conducted on similar lines, with the same degree of success. It was soon after this change had been effected that war between France and Russia was declared. This suggested the idea of a military spectacle, called *Les Cosaques*, which was performed with enormous success at the Porte St. Martin. The piece contained a national song that became very popular, and in composing a set of quadrilles, to which I gave the name of *Les Cosaques*, I introduced the famous melody. I sold it, as I had sold many compositions before, for 5*l*. Lafleur told me that he soon made a clear profit of

500*l.* by my quadrille. Fortunately for me, it was performed almost everywhere, and so an appreciable sum came to me in fees from the Society of Composers.

While I was conducting the orchestra at the Salle Ste. Cecile, I engaged, as principal viola, a clever young musician named Cantin, to whom a painful accident happened one night, when, between the parts, he was playing a game called "Toupie Hollandaise," which is a sort of table skittles. In spinning the top that was to knock down the skittles, the string became entangled somehow round the middle finger of poor Cantin's left hand, and his finger got so dreadfully torn, that it had to be amputated at once. Viola playing being now out of the question, this promising young musician had to set his wits to work and seek employment of another kind. He first became clerk at an agency, and when, a little later, the theatre *Folies-Dramatiques*, which had landed several proprietors in bankruptcy, was to be sold, Cantin, having got a little money together, bought the lease, and exerted himself to the utmost to make his new speculation pay. It was up-hill work for some time, but he happened to come across Lecocq, and though the composer was till then unknown, fortune, at once, smiled on both. Lecocq had just finished *La Fille de Madame Angot*, which he offered to Cantin for the *Folies-Dramatiques*. I need not recall what a long run this operette had in Paris, in the provinces, and, indeed, all over the world, for it is too well known to need recapitulation. *La Fille de Madame Angot*, which was a fortune in itself, was followed by *Madame*

Favart, *Giroflé-Giroflá*, *Les Cloches de Corneville*, *La Fille
du Tambour Major*, *La Mascotte*, besides other equally
successful works, and Cantin soon amassed an enormous
fortune, and was able to buy a splendid country residence
at St. Mandé near Paris.   He also built for himself the
magnificent house on the Boulevard Péreire which, for the
past few years, has been the residence of Sarah Bernhardt.
With a view to enjoying life thoroughly, Cantin set up a
pretty villa at the Cap d'Antibes on the shores of the
Mediterranean, and it is there I have been in the habit of
meeting him every winter, when I go in search of the
warmth not to be found in London or Paris.   In talking over
old times, Cantin, who, I regret to say, died in April last,
invariably declared that the loss of his finger was the
origin of his fortune, and so it practically was.   Fate works
very mysteriously sometimes !

In the year 1856 I became conductor of Le Jardin
d'Hiver, or Winter Garden, a magnificent establishment in
the Champs Elysées, where, with an orchestra of eighty
musicians, I had plenty of scope for the enterprise I
possessed.   One of my first projects was to organize
monster Sunday afternoon concerts, for which I engaged a
full military band to play in conjunction with my orchestra,
and as in addition I had first-class solo vocalists, these
concerts became the rage.   *Bals de nuit* were also frequently
given with a like success.   While I was conducting these
concerts at the Jardin d'Hiver, I carried out the novel idea
in one of my programmes of having a triple quartett of

slide trombones, that is to say, three players to each part. I was on very friendly terms, at the time, with Dieppo, the celebrated trombone player, who was principal at the Opéra, and professor at the Conservatoire. Dieppo, who was a native of Denmark, had come to Paris at a very early age, and soon attained. celebrity, becoming, in fact, the greatest trombone player that ever lived. Besides composing numerous solos, studies, exercises for his favourite instrument, he published a tutor for the slide trombone, which is still in general use, because it is considered the best on record. Chatting with Dieppo one day, I learnt he had arranged some trombone quartetts, and it occurred to me that I might make something of a sensation by introducing them at my concerts with three players to each part, making twelve in all. And as, for such a scheme, I needed good performers, I engaged only those who had obtained a first prize in Dieppo's class at the Conservatoire. My plan delighted the handsome Dane, and it was arranged that he should himself conduct on this occasion. The three pieces selected were the septuor from *Lucie*, the Fisherman's Prayer from *Masaniello*, and Johann Strauss's valse *Philomelen*. Playing a valse on a trombone was certainly a *tour de force*, but it was most successfully accomplished, and the performance was a triumph. I put the twelve trombone players in a semi-circle in the orchestra, -with Dieppo in the centre, and the effect was singularly striking. I am unable at this lapse of time, and having no notes to go upon, to recall the names of all the players, but

G

among them were Rome, Richir, Dantonnet, Simon, Vobaron junior, Venon, Puchot, François, Moreau and Sauret (father of Emile Sauret, the great violin player, professor at the London Academy). Many years after, I re-repeated this performance at the Alhambra, on the occasion of one of my annual benefits, but I did not again venture upon a valse. I replaced it by the quartett from *Rigoletto.*

It was also about the year 1856 that I made the acquaintance of Jacques Offenbach. The famous composer, who, as everybody knows, was a native of Germany, commenced his career in Paris as a violoncellist, this being the instrument he played at theatres and concerts on his first arrival in the French capital. When Loiseau resigned the post of *chef-d'orchestre* at the Théâtre Français Offenbach succeeded him, and it was whilst fulfilling this engagement he began composing short pieces as entr'acte music. Many of these compositions were both original and pretty, terms that are not always interchangeable, and their author speedily became a celebrity. Amongst the earliest successes of Offenbach was a one-act operette called *Pepito*, that he had been specially commissioned to write for the Variétés Théâtre. The popularity of this operette was entirely due to the music, and it was followed in a very short time by *Les Deux Aveugles*, which was also a musical success.

Offenbach then left the Théâtre Français for Les Folies Marigny, a small theatre in the Champs Elysées, where his operettes were exclusively performed. And subsequently he was appointed director and conductor of the Bouffets

Parisiens, a position he held for a great number of years, to the delight of the public that rushed to hear his works, and also much to his own profit, for he soon amassed a considerable fortune. Like most talented men, Offenbach had an unequal disposition, as an incident that occurred to myself will illustrate. It so happened that for one of my Sunday afternoon concerts at the Jardin d'Hiver, I wanted to engage a popular singer named Darcier, who was at the time fulfilling an engagement with Offenbach. I wrote in the usual way to ask the maestro for his permission, and this was so cordially granted, that I at once advertised Darcier's name largely in the newspapers, and on the posters as one of the principal attractions of my concert. Great was my surprise, therefore, to learn from Darcier, the day before the date fixed for the entertainment, that Offenbach had forbidden him to sing for me. Not in the best of tempers I called in the evening to see Offenbach at the stage door of the theatre, and asked him for an explanation, but, as this was not forthcoming, and as my rage, I suppose, was increasing, from words we soon came to blows. It was an undignified scrimmage, of course, as all such scrimmages are but, in moments of passion men sometimes lose self-control. Except that we each had to look for our hats that had rolled upon the floor, to set our collars in order, and pick up the spectacles that each had lost, no serious results ensued from the undignified scuffle that had taken place. I did not, however, see anything of Offenbach for some years; not, in fact, until I met him at the Alhambra in London,

G 2

when, as he made the first advance towards me, by offering me his hand, we agreed to let bygones be bygones. After that we were the best of friends, our friendship lasting to the hour of his death.

CHAPTER VI.

Concert at the Jardin d'Hiver on the anniversary of the Prince
Imperial's birth—A mark of Imperial favour—A family
bereavement—M. Daudé—Fête at Asnières—Departure for
Brussels—Touring concerts in Belgium—Gambling losses
at Spa—Break up of tour—Sailing for England.

WHAT was spoken of at the time as the grandest concert that
had ever been given in Paris was the fête I organized at the
Jardin d'Hiver in March, 1857, on the anniversary of the
Prince Imperial's birth.   I enlarged my stringed orchestra
for the occasion to 200 musicians, and obtained, moreover,
permission from Maréchal Magnan, who was in command
of the garrison of Paris, for all the bands of the various
regiments—infantry, cavalry, and artillery—garrisoned in
town and in the forts, to take part in the concert.   The
letter written by order of Maréchal Magnan, in which he gave
me his consent, is one of the few documents I have preserved.
It runs thus :—

MONSIEUR,

   Le Maréchal Magnan me charge d'avoir l'honneur de vous
informer qu'il a donné les ordres nécessaires pour que dimanche
prochain au Jardin d'Hiver, toutes les musiques de la garnison

de Paris et des forts environnants vous prêtent le concours que vous désirez.

Recevez, Monsieur, l'assurance de ma consideration distinguée.

Le Capitaine aide-de-camp,

COMTE DE CLERMONT TONNERRE.

In preparation for this event I had composed a military quadrille, called *La Guerre*, which was an allusion of course to the siege of Sebastopol.   I had all the parts published by Lafleur, and printed on cards for distribution amongst the bands, and there being an important part for bugles in the quadrille, I had to get permission for the Clairons des Zouaves de la Garde to attend.   The forty drums, also needed, were forthcoming, with a tambour-major in command, and, at the suggestion of Maréchal Magnan, a detachment of a hundred Grenadiers de la Garde was posted outside the concert room ; these men, at a signal from me, and with a view to increasing the effect, firing blank cartridges in the air during the last figure in the quadrille.   We had a long rehearsal on the preceding day, and the performance, which went very smoothly, was a tremendous success, 10,000 persons attending.   Another piece I composed, also, for this concert, was a cantata entitled *Hymne à la Gloire*, the words of which, couched in thrilling and martial language, were written by a member of Parliament, M. de Belmontet, one of the intimates of the first Napoleon, and the poet who was considered the Poet Laureate of France under Napoleon III.   Darcier sang the four verses, and I introduced in the finale the *Partant pour la*

Syrie, which was at the time the national air of France. All the military bands joined the orchestra in this piece to the number of 1200, and it had the honour of an encore. The Emperor and Empress were present at the performance, and the sight of the Winter Garden, resplendent with the brilliant military uniforms of the gentlemen, and the dazzling display of diamonds on the part of the ladies, was of the most imposing kind. The next day an equerry drove up in one of the Imperial carriages to my door, to present me, on the part of their Majesties, with a signet ring in commemoration of the event. I have worn this ring on my left hand ever since. In passing I may here recall the fact that the Emperor and Empress had undertaken to act as sponsors to all the children born in France on the same day as the Prince Imperial. No fewer than 3834 notifications of birth were sent in, a number known to be in excess of those actually born on the day, and I was assured some years ago that most of these god-children had, at different times, and in various ways, sought Imperial assistance or protection. One, however whose baptismal certificate I know bears date March 16th, 1856, has not only never solicited imperial help, but has, unaided, attained a certain celebrity. I refer to Gangloff, the composer of popular songs, whose speciality it happens to be to write for Paulus of café concert renown.

The mark of imperial favour of which I had been the recipient after my concert, did much no doubt to dispel the gloom that had been cast over me and my family by the harsh treatment of which my cousin Auguste Rivière had been the victim after the Coup d'Etat in 1851. This cousin, who was an *avocat* by profession, and a Republican by conviction, had attained much celebrity in defending conspirators against the Empire in the Courts of Justice, and when the Coup d'Etat took place, he was arrested and taken to a cell at the fort of Bicêtre, where, in spite of such attention as we were able to bestow upon him, and which comprised sending a man to him daily with a can of good soup, he suffered terribly during his captivity from the severity of the weather. At the trial, despite all argument, Auguste Rivière was condemned to transportation, and it was not until he had been sent to Brest, to be in readiness for embarking for La Guyane, that the result of the efforts made by the Archbishop of Paris, who interceded with the Emperor, and by my mother, who appealed to her godmother, the Duchesse d'Uzes, were communicated to the poor captive, who was ultimately released, and brought back to Paris, only, however, to die a few months after from shock to the nervous system. Pleasant memories of this clever barrister, whose life was thus shortened, have remained in the Rivière family ; memories that are cherished in particular by his sister Armande, a woman who was a great beauty in her time, and who is now the widowed Comtesse de Chabet, her husband, the Comte Chassaing de Chabet, having died soon after the German invasion of Paris in 1870, when their residence at Puteaux was destroyed by the firing of the German army.

I became acquainted in the early fifties with M. Daudé, the manager of the Jardin d'Hiver, a clever and affable man, who was also a good musician, and the particulars of whose early career may interest some of my readers. From being a chorister boy at the church of St. Sulpice, Daudé soon developed exceptional talent, and becoming leading baritone at the Opera Comique, he, with Ponchard the tenor and Madame Casimir the soprano, made a great hit in Herold's *Pré aux clercs*. Retaining this position, Daudé, who had married the daughter of Mayo, the music publisher, seemed to be on the high road to fortune, when his professional career was suddenly blighted in the saddest manner conceivable. Returning with his wife on a cold winter's day from St. Germain, he had the misfortune to see her crushed to death before his eyes by a fall as she was alighting from the train at the Gare St. Lazare. The poor fellow caught such a chill as he stood bareheaded over his wife's grave that his vocal strings became affected, and, from that day Daudé was never able to sing another note of music. He became in turn manager of concert halls and theatres, and after that, his integrity being proverbial, he was given a position of considerable trust at the Maisons-Lafitte and other racecourses. In this last-named capacity Daudé made a fortune rapidly, and he passed the last years of his life at Chatou, dying at the ripe age of 85.

It was whilst Daudé was manager of the Jardin d'Hiver that I first made his acquaintance, and it was also at this building that success tempted me, as success has tempted many ambitious mortals before me, to further ventures, and in one of these I lost all the money I had been able to save. I took the château and park of Asnières for a grand summer fête, calling it the Foire aux Plaisirs. The preparations comprised a monster concert, a ball with military bands, balloon ascents, boating, races, fireworks, in short, all kinds of amusements. In advertisements alone I had expended a small fortune. The day opened well, a good number of people passing the turnstiles early in the day; but it was evident, the day being Sunday, that the majority of visitors were reserving themselves for the evening fête, and this was completely marred by a terrific storm that broke out at six o'clock and lasted for hours. Utterly discouraged, I left Daudé, my friend and partner, to pay all he could with the gate money in hand, whilst, in despair, I repaired to our hotel to await the news on his return. This money loss was a sad blow to me; and as with it came a domestic trouble of an irreparable nature, and to which I have already referred, sick at heart I hastily packed my trunks, and in twenty-four hours' time found myself in Brussels, entirely without funds, and, what was even worse, without any set project for my future. Sympathizing letters and money help soon, however, came pouring in upon me from various relatives, and, on meeting by chance young Meissonnier, the son of one of the leading music publishers in Paris, we arranged to organize some monster concerts in the principal towns of Belgium, Meissonnier himself undertaking to provide the capital and take the responsibilities of

management, whilst I was to be *chef-d'orchestre*, and to share
with him all profits accruing from the venture. The scheme
was at once started, and I wrote off to Lafleur to send me
the band parts of my quadrille, *La Guerre*, and also the
Hymne à la Gloire. We commenced operations at Brussels by getting the permission of the burgomaster to hold a
concert in the park, for admission to which a franc was to
be charged. This proposal being without precedent, the
burgomaster had first to consult his colleagues, and when
the concession was made in our favour, there was a stipula-
tion that one-fourth of the receipts should be devoted to
the poor of Brussels. We obtained also the sanction of
the general commanding the army in Brussels for all the
bands to appear at our concert, upon our paying a hundred
francs to each ; and after arranging with the different band-
masters, the next thing that occupied our attention was the
orchestra. This involved rather more difficulty, but ultimately we came to terms with the orchestra of the opera at
the Théâtre de la Monnaie. Whilst I attended to the
rehearsals, Meissonnier was busy with the advertisements,
and everything seemed to promise well for our concert, for
which we had a tremendous platform erected on the large
basin in the centre of the park. Being in Belgium, instead
of Paris, I substituted *Lä Brabançonne* for *Partant pour la
Syrie* in my *Hymne à la Gloire*. The weather this time
was propitious, and on settling accounts, after we had paid
all expenses, we were left with 40*l.* to divide, which we
considered a good start.

From Brussels we went to Ostend, to hold a similar concert there; but this time we encountered more difficulty in
finding a suitable place, and we ultimately decided to erect
a platform on a piece of land adjoining the public promenade by the sea front, obtaining permission of the colonel
commanding the line regiment in garrison at Ostend to let
a company attend the concert, and prevent people from
passing along that part of the promenade in front of the
band-stand without payment.   A *contretemps* unfortunately
occurred that necessitated the postponement of the concert
from the date originally fixed.   This arose from Meissonnier, Choudens, and myself being poisoned by some
mussels we ate at a restaurant luncheon.   When, however
the following week, we were busy again with our plans, the
burgomaster informed us that we could not have the company of soldiers promised by the colonel, for the promenade must not be stopped.   We learnt, moreover, that the
sailors in the lower part of the town had threatened to
smash everything if their passage along the sea front was in
any way impeded.   Having sold reserved seats enough at
three francs each to cover expenses, we decided to run the
gauntlet, and when the day came we hired all the bathing
machines, and with them made a sort of wall at each end
near the orchestra.   All to no purpose, for when the hour
to begin the concert drew near, the mob had taken possession of the reserved front seats, and everything was con-
fusion.   We did the best we could under such trying

circumstances, but in settling up matters there was only a very small profit to share.

From Ostend we journeyed to Spa, where gambling was largely practised at the Kursall in those days. Here we selected the Rond-Point of the Promenade for our concert, making arrangements, at a moderate price, to have the orchestra belonging to the Casino, in addition to military bands from Liège, Gand, Namur, and Louvain. Fortunately, we paid many of our expenses in advance. I say fortunately, for, after the manner of many foolish visitors to a gambling city, we were stupid enough to fill in our spare time at the roulette tables. I am not sure that I was not idiot enough to think we had discovered a wonderful system, merely because for a day or two I managed to win 6l. or 8l. It is hardly necessary, I suppose, to say that my system landed me where other systems have landed players; namely, in complete loss. This was my plan:—Black having won six times, I staked on red, doubling the stake each time. In about ten minutes Meissonnier and I were literally cleared out, black having come up twenty-two times in succession. And it was on the eve of our concert that we found ourselves leaving the Casino and going out at night into the fresh air without a coin in our pockets. We had a good attendance at the concert, but our losses at roulette, which amounted to 300l., made us decide to dissolve partnership. Meissonnier, consequently, returned to Paris, and I stayed on at Spa till my friend

Daudé let me know how matters were going on at home. Acting on my behalf, he had paid my creditors in Paris 13½ per cent.; and the whole of the remainder, I may here state, was paid by me as soon as I made the money. I thus got rid of all my indebtedness, without, I may add, a single debt of any kind, small or large, being pressed for by anybody. After staying for a time with the family of M. Marquet, an architect of Spa, I decided to leave these new friends and try my luck in London. I sailed for England in November, 1857, embarking from Antwerp in the boat called the *Baron Osy*, in which, I remember, I had a very rough crossing that lasted twenty-four hours.

PART II.—ENGLAND.

CHAPTER I.

Arrival in London—General impressions of the Great City—
 Learning English—Renewal of acquaintance with Jullien—
 Berlioz's opinion about Jullien—Hymn of Universal Harmony—Julien's decline—His return to Paris—His madness
 and tragic end.

IT was on a cold, foggy, and depressing November morning
that I landed at the docks in London. My English
vocabulary consisted of about half a dozen words. I
was glad, therefore, on leaving the boat to meet with
someone with whom I could converse, and as my
fellow-traveller, who was a German, addressed me in
French and volunteered to assist me, I gladly accepted
his offer by asking him to recommend me to an
hotel in a central position, where I could have a room
at a moderate cost. Assuring me that he knew just
the place to suit me, I had my luggage put on the top of a
cab, and was duly conducted by my Teutonic guide to an
hotel in the Commercial Road, Whitechapel. What a long
drive it seemed, to be sure! And what a place it was
when we got there! It was a small, dirty-looking hotel,
kept also by a German who could speak French. On

H

being ushered into a room, I was offered one of three beds, but when I learnt that one of them was occupied by a sailor, and that the other would probably be let before night, I preferred (a room to myself, I found upon inquiry, being impossible) to pay for the bed, and to decline occupying it. Consequently I had my luggage once more put upon a cab and tried my luck this time in Leicester Square, a neighbourhood I had long heard of. I managed, without much difficulty, to make the cabman understand it was an hotel I wanted, and ultimately I was set down at the New York Hotel, where a by no means luxurious room was allotted to me at the top of the building. The fatigues of the journey, and the dreary drive through bustling London streets, having induced sleep, I went to bed directly after dinner, and slept for twenty-four hours, waking only once to look at my watch, and then making a mistake of twelve hours, by thinking it was 4 a.m. when it was 4 o'clock in the afternoon, albeit the practising of somersaults by a family of acrobats was going on in an adjoining room. Refreshed by this long spell of rest, I went down to dinner, and sallied forth afterwards on my first stroll in the streets of London. Antony Lamotte, an old friend of mine, was, I remembered to have heard, conductor of the orchestra at the Argyll Rooms, where also Boulcourt, who had played under me in Paris, was engaged as first cornet. I learnt, however, upon inquiry, that owing to the dancing licence being withdrawn from the Argyll Rooms, the proprietor, Mr. Bignell, had transferred the business to the Adelaide Gallery, where the Gatti restaurant is now situated, and it was here I ultimately found Lamotte and Boulcourt, too, both of whom welcomed me heartily to London and asked me to meet them after the performance. To kill time, I tucked myself up in a quiet corner in the gallery at the end of the hall, and I must have got drowsy again, for, when the building was closed and the waiters were turning out the gas, I was roused by one of them, who inquired what I was doing there. " Waiting for Lamotte and Boulcourt," I replied, and on being told they had left, I set out for my hotel again, which I reached in the pelting rain. The next day I determined to have a long walk, with a view, of course, to comparing London with Paris, and, armed with a pocket dictionary, as well as the " Guide to London," that accompanies so many Frenchmen on their travels, I started forth on my lonely wanderings. Of course I noticed a deal to make me think the metropolis rather a topsy-turvy sort of city, the vehicles, for one thing, being driven on what was, to me, the wrong side of the road. I found cause also for remark in the soldiers' dress, the jackets being red and the trousers blue in England, whereas, in France, the trousers are red and the jackets blue. I am not, by any means, saying that I criticized the appearance of the troops. On the contrary, I well remember that the stalwart and magnificent bearing of the men belonging to the Horse Guards made upon me, as they must make upon all foreigners, a great impression. Where, of course, I committed a stupid mistake, was in supposing that a pocket dictionary could help me to learn English. But I am probably not the first Frenchman by hundreds who has looked in his dictionary for the translation of chop-house, oil and colourman, or wines from the wood without getting any further forward in his English. Indeed, the further I travelled the less I seemed to understand, and fearing to make a muddle of my English in speaking it, I used to carry a card with "Trafalgar Square" written plainly upon it. This, when I lost myself, I showed to a policeman, and as I did so often without speaking a word, I was more than once taken for a dumb person, and directed to the point I wanted by signs and motions. I am bound to confess that this wounded me very much, and, so I resolved to give up my dictionary and phrase book, and take lessons in English at once. In my eagerness to learn the language quickly I asked the professor I engaged to give me conversational lessons, rather than the usual rudimentary exercises adopted for beginners, and this course of study involved me in some blunders that sent my tutor sometimes into fits of laughter. For instance, when I was explaining that I intended organizing some concerts, he asked me who would manage them for me, to which I replied, that I should be the undertaker myself. And it took the poor man some minutes to make me understand that the word "undertaker" only applied to funerals.

When I had been in London a few days, and had had time to turn myself round, I called upon Jullien, who was

then conducting promenade concerts at Her Majesty's
Theatre. His engagements for the season being complete,
he was unable to offer me a position in his orchestra, but,
of music copying, at which I was an expert, he gave me
more than I could conveniently undertake, and, as I re-
newed acquaintance with several of my old Paris friends,
who were in Jullien's orchestra, including Jullien Tolbecque, Collinet, Remusat, Lavigne, and others, life in
the metropolis opened for me quite auspiciously. I was
on the free list at Her Majesty's, and consequently spent
most of my evenings there. The popular vocalist of
that season was, I remember, a German lady, named
Jetty Treffz, a brilliant soprano, who subsequently married
Johann Strauss, of Vienna. The Belgian clarinette player,
Wilde, was also creating a sensation at the time. It was
just after the fall of Lucknow, and Jullien, who, as I have
already stated, knew so well how to turn every chance to
account, hit the public taste with his famous Indian quadrille,
which contained some cleverly-arranged Indian melodies.
This was performed every evening, and proved a remarkable success. And his *Fern leaves* valse, composed about
the same time, was scarcely less popular than the Indian
quadrille. Not content, however, with doing well during
the winter, the noted *chéf-d'orchestre* took the Surrey
Gardens for a series of summer concerts, and here he
managed to lose the money made at Her Majesty's.
Pursuing his spirit of enterprise, Jullien started touring in
the principal towns in England, touring, it must be re-

membered, not being as general in the early fifties as it is
at this end of the century.   His secretary at that time
was his first horn player, Mr. Jarrett, who afterwards
became a popular impresario in New York, where he made
a large fortune.   In the summer of 1853, Jullien took his
complete orchestra with him to New York, where he had
an enormous success at the Castle Gardens in that
city.   He was unanimously praised by the critics everywhere in the States—Washington, Baltimore, Boston, and
Philadelphia all being visited in turn.   He came back to
England, covered with glory, and had also a good share
of dollars in his pockets, most of which, however, with the
extravagance inherent in his nature, were devoted to the
purchase of a pretty estate near Brussels, where he spent
about six weeks in the spring of each year.   This went on
for a few years, but subsequently the pretty Belgian residence
was sold, to provide funds for a Drury Lane season, and the
production at his own expense of his opera *Peter the Great.*
The mounting of this work ruined Jullien financially, and
he was compelled to accept engagements as conductor of
concerts.   His large music shop in Regent Street was also
a failure, but the more modest enterprise of the flower-
stall held at her husband's concerts by Madame Jullien,
where bouquets à la Jullien were freely sold, proved a
profitable source of revenue.   Jullien's last season in
London took place, I remember, at the Lyceum in
1858, but the once popular leader's success was on the
wane.

Berlioz,[1] who knew Jullien well, speaks of him in his memoirs in the following terms :—

"I shall not enter into details as to my first stay in England, for they are simply interminable. . . . . I was engaged by Jullien, the celebrated director of the promenade concerts, to conduct the orchestra of a grand English opera, which he had the wild ambition of establishing at Drury Lane Theatre. Jullien, in his incontestable and uncontested character of madman, had engaged a splendid orchestra, a first-rate chorus, and a very fair set of singers ; he had forgotten nothing but the repertoire. The sole work he had in view was an opera he had ordered from Balfe, called *The Maid of Artois*, and he proposed to open his series with an English translation of *Lucia di Lammermoor*. While they were waiting for the *mise-en-scène* of Balfe's opera, he would have had to take 400*l*. a night to barely cover the expenses of " Lucia." The result was inevitable. The receipts from " Lucia " never came near 400*l*. Balfe's opera was only a moderate success, and in a very short time Jullien was ruined. I never touched a penny beyond my first month's salary, notwithstanding all the fine protestations of Jullien, who, after all, was doubtless as honest a man as he could be, consistently with such a depth of folly as his. Jullien seriously proposed to me to get up the opera of *Robert le Diable* in six days, though he had neither copies, nor translation, nor dresses, nor scenery, and though the singers did not know a note of

[1] By kind permission of Macmillan and Co.